INTO THE BLUE

Recent Titles by Gerald Hammond from Severn House

FINE TUNE
FLAMESCAPE
INTO THE BLUE
A RUNNING JUMP

INTO THE BLUE

Gerald Hammond

This first world edition published in Great Britain 2000 by
SEVERN HOUSE PUBLISHERS LTD of
9–15 High Street, Sutton, Surrey SM1 1DF.
This first world edition published in the U.S.A. 2000 by
SEVERN HOUSE PUBLISHERS INC of
595 Madison Avenue, New York, N.Y. 10022.

British Library Cataloguing in Publication Data

Hammond,   Gerald,   1926-
Into the blue
1.Love stories
I. Title
823.9'14 [F]

ISBN 0-7278-5509-3

Typeset by Palimpsest Book Production Ltd.,
Polmont, Stirlingshire, Scotland.
Printed and bound in Great Britain by
MPG Books Ltd, Bodmin, Cornwall.

Author's Note

Never having had a daughter, I was wary of using young girls as characters in my books. (I except Deborah Calder, who anyway was a tomboy.)

More recently, having been blessed with five grand-daughters now aged between the cradle and the university (with accompanying daughters-in-law), I felt more able to cope with these remarkable persons. At the same time I was becoming aware of and irritated by inappropriate use of the expression 'girl power'. I was then attracted to the subject of a young woman being drawn into a traditionally male activity and making a go of it.

This is the fourth book in which I have set off along that road with only the faintest idea where it would lead. Two turned themselves into crime stories, but this is not one of them. If the reader gets half as much fun from reading it as I had in writing it, I shall be more than satisfied.

This book is therefore affectionately dedicated to

Naomi, Laura, Lyndsey, Stephanie and Sunita.

I am also indebted to my son David for his considerable help with the gliding sequences. I should add that these are the only real people who have any counterparts, however approximate, in the story.

One

Colin Fergusson lost his wife in a hotel fire shortly after his fortieth birthday. Ironically, she had been attending her own mother's funeral. He would have been with her, but their occasional child-minders had been unavailable and it had been agreed that he would stay at home and look after their young daughter, the sole product of their marriage.

The change to his life might have been devastating. They had been married for sixteen years which, if not wholly ecstatic, had been quietly contented. And he now had sole responsibility for a three-year-old daughter, christened Aimée but invariably known as Amy.

As befitted a successful meteorologist he was of a quietly logical turn of mind, occasionally illuminated by sudden bursts of intuition. A few days after his wife's funeral, when the sense of having been cast adrift in an open boat had begun to subside and after Amy was settled and asleep, he shut himself in his study with a bottle of whisky and considered his situation. He could, he supposed, engage some kind of housekeeper and continue to commute to his work, as senior forecaster for a television network with periodic detours to lecture or to appear in television commercials. Like many other men who had come late to fatherhood, he regarded his daughter, this mysterious infant materialised from his own genes, with awe and uncertainty. A nodding acquaintance with certain television pundits made while waiting to make his own appearances with the weather had convinced him that this would not be a good upbringing and that, while no great harm would be done by a boarding school, a parent, especially a single parent, should be around throughout the school holidays, ready to give advice and comfort, and should convey a sense of permanent security by being *there*, at home and in theory available during term-time.

On the other hand, he could become one of the vast army of the wholly self-employed. At first glance, this seemed an unpropitious idea. Meteorologists are nearly always salaried. But much of the time inescapably spent standing by for the Met Office to divulge the latest data had been spent in developing his own version of the computer programs used for extrapolating the weather to come from that which had gone before. He had built into it the accumulated experience culled from the weather records of many years and would no doubt continue to improve on it for years to come. He was not the first to undertake such an exercise but he had been lucky or clever. His forecasts were, on average, more accurate and more detailed than those of his rivals and extended further ahead with a reasonable chance of accuracy. Commercial bodies, sports organisers, sailing and flying magazines and a variety of others to whom advance warning of the weather was essential appreciated his willingness to express his forecasts in terms of percentage probabilities.

They had taken to consulting him over the phone and, to his surprise, had no objection to paying a fee for his assistance, especially for a forecast specific to their local areas. If he became self-employed, perhaps their patronage would continue. He might even retain enough income and gain the time to enjoy to the full his one passion, gliding, though whether funds would be available for that as well as for boarding school was open to doubt. On balance, he was advised by one of the new brood of TV agony aunts, family life would outweigh any deficiency of formal education.

After some months of unsatisfactory experiences with a variety of home helps – mostly bumbling or dirty, dishonest or flirtatious, and one who attempted to trap him into a second marriage – he took the plunge.

To his surprise (for he was a modest man) his former clients stayed with him and word of mouth brought him new business. He was also lucky. His forecast of freak winds of hurricane strength in the Irish Sea, not anticipated by any of his rivals, saved his contacts a great deal of money and, by causing the postponement of a major sailing regatta, probably some lives as well. The resultant publicity brought a minor rush of new clients.

His new lifestyle suited him well. Instead of commuting to the city to be at the beck and call of others, he could breakfast early, digitise the latest readings from the Met Office into his computer and fax his forecast to the many subscribers who wanted daily predictions. He remained in touch with several hundred amateur weather stations from which he could obtain more detailed local figures when required, in return for which he circulated a newsletter which also included less well-known titbits of weather lore. It remained only to answer any more specific queries – the best day for a fete in Clacton or the chance of snow for skiing in the Cairngorms – and he was free. All of the cleaning, most of the laundry and some of the cooking were dealt with by Mrs Briggs, who lived a hundred yards along the street. The remaining chores he could manage in short time, leaving himself available for the garden, for Amy or for his gliding. Mrs Briggs had a teenage daughter, Celandine, recently liberated from school but not yet favoured by any employer, who was always glad to earn a little money by watching over Amy.

Time, as is its habit, slipped away. Celandine Briggs found a part-time job stacking shelves in the local supermarket and was less often available for Amy-sitting. But by then Amy, adjudged still too delicate a flower for boarding school, was at the local school and for the middle of most days her father could indulge his passion for gliding as often as the weather and his pocket would permit. During school holidays he was prepared to make the supreme sacrifice, but Amy was always ready to help him in the garden and she was often invited to spend time in the houses of her school-friends, thus liberating him for a visit to the nearby gliding club.

It had been impressed on Mr Fergusson that he must try never to frustrate the child, so although he was not always enraptured to find a slim figure at his elbow and to be asked, "What are you doing, Daddy?" nevertheless he would defer his work and patiently explain about lenticulars and rotor clouds. If his discourse tended to drift in the direction of thermals and wave systems, that was only natural. Usually Amy would wander off after a few minutes and leave him to finish his work.

Mr Fergusson tried to converse with his daughter as often as he could, though it was hard going at times. Both were to remember in particular their conversation of one Sunday afternoon. He was about to make his escape, leaving Amy in the care of Celandine.

"Where are you going, Daddy?" six-year-old Amy asked him.

"I'm going gliding."

There was a pause. "You go there a lot. What's gliding?"

"Sort of flying," he said.

Amy looked doubtfully at a passing sparrow. "You can fly?"

"Not like that. You take a good look at a bird. So that their muscles can work their wings, they have enormous chests."

"Like Mrs Briggs?"

Mr Fergusson closed his eyes, swallowed and shook his head. "No, not like Mrs Briggs. They have big ribcages to give their muscles leverage. We aren't built like that, so we have to use machines."

"Aeroplanes?"

"Gliders are like aeroplanes except that they don't have engines. You have to be clever and use the . . . wind. You must have seen the gliders from the club, they come over here often enough. Not the noisy ones – they're the tow-planes. The gliders are the slim, quiet ones."

"Can I come with you?"

Mr Fergusson bit back a sharp answer. Amy was a good child, but all young children fiddle with things, as part of the process of learning. He could image small hands moving the airbrake lever or the canopy lock at a critical moment. Or even a sudden demand for the toilet. "When you're bigger," he said, "I'll be happy to take you up and we'll have a lot of fun together."

From then on, Amy took note of the slender shapes drifting across the sky. Until then, they had been part of the scenery and of no more significance than the clouds.

The Fergussons lived in a medium-sized but well-appointed old house on the edge of what was still referred to as a village although it had grown slowly over the years to a size at which most would have considered it a small town.

Colin had several times considered moving to a location close to a good day-school. But this would have meant moving away from the airstrip. Also, theirs was a favoured location. The cottages that comprised most of the street and which, while not thatched-roofed, looked as though they were meant to be were separated from them by a small market garden. Across the road was the beginning of open farmland. On the other, or non-village, side were the park and gardens of a large house, almost a mansion. The house had been built by a general who, following on a famous but now forgotten victory in some remote corner of the Empire, had expected a grateful country to mark the occasion by making generous provision for his old age. The country had proved rather less grateful than he had anticipated and the house had passed through many hands, being in turn a lunatic asylum, a nursing home and a retirement home for ageing civil servants. Back in private hands, the house and grounds were meticulously maintained although the owner, who was an industrialist and understood to be fabulously wealthy, was usually in London or with his wife in the south of France. The house which Mr Fergusson owned and occupied had once been a sort of dower house, built at the same time as Downfield Hall by the general as a refuse dump for unwanted female relatives.

The head gardener on the estate, along with his colleague the semi-retired gamekeeper, gently dissuaded the locals from making too free with the grounds but, because Celandine was walking out with the head gardener's younger son (employed as a very junior gardener), her presence was tolerated or at least a blind eye was turned. Amy became accustomed to wandering the estate freely while Celandine, on her days off, exchanged sighs and hand-clasps with her boyfriend. As a buffer between the well-tended lawns and gardens close to the house and the home farm was a broad stretch of parkland scattered with stands of tall specimen trees. The grass was kept cropped by sheep but no other agriculture was allowed to intrude.

On a blessedly mild but bright day in the summer when Amy was seven, she was sitting on a wooden bench against the south wall of a summerhouse and looking peevishly at the lake. She was bored. She was not of an age to appreciate the beauty of a placid lake reflecting tall cedar trees, nor to thrill to the occasional splash of a trout. There were two gliders within sight overhead but they still had little meaning for her unless she thought that her Daddy might be in one of them. They were stubbornly refusing to do anything interesting.

"Hello," said a voice. "What are you doing here?"

Living with a scientist had given Amy a literal turn of mind. "I'm not exactly doing anything," she said. "Except sitting. Is sitting doing something?"

The boy took a seat at the extreme other end of the bench and they sat in silence for a moment while he pondered the question. "Yes," the boy said firmly at last. "Because if you're sitting you're also breathing and thinking and your heart's beating and your blood's going round and . . . and so on. Unless you're dead, of course. Then you could be sitting and not doing anything. I'm Anthony Hope-Williams but you can call me Tony. I'm eight."

"I'm Amy Fergusson," Amy said. "You can call me Amy. I live *there*." She pointed to where the roof of Firhaven showed through the trees. "And I'm seven."

She slid on her bottom along the bench and they solemnly shook hands. Tony was slightly taller than she was, she found when they stood up. He had fair hair and blue eyes, which made her slightly envious because that month she had rather a fancy for growing into a statuesque and glamorous blonde, like a lady she had seen on television, instead of being skinny and having chestnut curls and brown eyes.

"Do you live here?" Amy asked.

Tony had to consider again. "Sometimes," he said at last. "My dad owns the house."

"You're not usually here, especially in summer," she said.

He shook his head. "We have a flat in London and a villa in the south of France. Dad likes it here but my mother can't stand the place. I think she expected the villagers to tug their forelocks and they won't do it."

"They probably would if she asked them," Amy said.

"I don't think so. They call her Lady Muck behind her back. I've heard them. And now something's happening," he said. "A divorce."

Amy was not quite sure what a divorce was, but from overheard snatches of adult conversation she was fairly sure that it was something undesirable if not disastrous. "That's a shame," she said.

"Yes. I'll probably have to spend a lot of my hols with Mum in Saint Tropez. It's boring there as well as being too hot. I'd rather be here. It's not just that there's much more to do, but my Mum doesn't let me do much in case I fall in or hurt myself or something. I can do pretty much what I want here. Do you fish?"

"I don't know," she said. "I've never tried."

As soon as she spoke she realised that what she had said made no sense. He looked at her with superior disdain. "I'm going to fish. You can watch me if you like." He took a key from his pocket and opened the door of the shed. There were several rods and some other interesting looking gear neatly arranged on the walls. He collected a long-handled net and a short, light, carbon-fibre rod which was already set up. He looked knowledgeably at the black, red and silver fly. "Butcher," he said. "That'll do." They walked down to the lakeside.

"I'm not supposed to come here unless somebody's with me."

"Well then—"

"But there is somebody with me. You are."

Amy was surprised to find that she counted as a person for supervisory purposes but she had more sense than to say so. She watched as Tony stripped some line off the reel and after a few false casts managed to put the line on the water, more or less straight.

"What are you fishing for?" she asked.

"Trout. Brown trout. My dad doesn't approve of rainbows. He says they're not a native species, they believe anything you throw at them and anyway they don't breed here in the wild. I'm going to prep school soon. As a boarder. What school are you at?"

"I'm at the local school but I'm going to Bath Ladies' College as a boarder next year."

Tony looked doubtful but continued to fish without comment. Amy watched. Often more may be learned by watching than by doing. Sometimes Tony cast well but more often the line fell in swirls on the water. From his better casts she judged that the secret was in the timing. When he let the line straighten behind him, it went out well; otherwise it was a mess. Also, he was casting out horizontally or even slightly upwards from the rod-tip so that the line was beginning to rebound before it settled. Seen from below, it would be enough to scare any fish. When he cast slightly downward, the line settled gently on the water. She wondered if she should tell him but decided that he would probably take offence.

"There's nothing moving," Tony said at last. "I wish I

could reach that patch of weed. That's where they'll be on a day like this. They like the shade because they don't have eyelids and they dazzle easily. That's what Mr Symonds says. He used to be the keeper here but he's more or less retired now."

"I know him," Amy said. "He lives in one of those cottages on the other side of my house."

"He makes his own beer." Tony cast again. The fly fell ten feet short of the weed which spread like a shadow across the water a stone's throw away.

"May I try?" Amy asked.

"Girls don't fish," he said, but then he relented. "Go ahead then. You can't catch less than I'm catching."

He drew the fly back in a series of twitches, letting the recovered line fall in loops in the grass at their feet. Amy took the rod. The cork handle was warm and sweaty from his hand. At first, the line refused to run out until she realised that she was standing on a loop of it. Then it seemed to go anywhere but where she wanted and Tony withdrew to a safe distance. "You're going to hook yourself," he said with satisfaction.

"I'm *not!*" she retorted. Gradually the timing came to her and she found the trick of keeping her cast down. She drew a little more line off the reel and put some energy into her cast. The line straightened just above the water and the fly settled at the edge of the weed, bobbing invitingly in the faintest of breezes.

For a long moment, nothing happened. Amy began to draw the fly back. It resisted.

"You're into the weed," said Tony.

There was an explosion in the water, or so it seemed.

11

The line went tight, the rod bowed and the reel emitted a single screech.

"Keep him out of the weed," Tony cried. Amy leaned back against the rod. It seemed impossible that such slender nylon as the leader could hold such a submarine, but the spring of the rod gave the fish no purchase, the knots held, the line survived. The rod bucked. The taut line moved around, apparently by magic, as the fish, still invisible below the now ruffled surface, headed away to the side.

"Keep the rod *up!*"

Amy did as she was bid, at the same time backing away from the water. Fumbling with the unfamiliar apparatus, she even managed to recover a little line.

"Shall I take over?" Tony asked anxiously.

Amy shook her head. She had got this far and she was going the rest of the way. It would not be really and truly her fish if somebody else landed it. Tony understood. The duties of a host had been drummed into him. He held the net in the water and Amy, still backing away, drew the fish nearer until, suddenly, it was in the net and on the bank.

"What is it?" she asked.

"Brown trout. A beauty!" he said generously. "Do you want to keep it or shall we put it back?"

The idea of returning her fish to the water was not to be contemplated. Amy wanted the whole world to admire her triumph over an elusive quarry. "I'd like to keep it," she said. "Please."

"Wait here a minute." He darted back to the hut.

Amy crouched down to admire her beautiful fish, now gasping in the dry air. She wished there was something she could do for it. The fish could not have been firmly hooked, because the hook had already fallen out of its mouth.

Tony dashed back with a priest – in this case an ebony rod weighted with lead at one end, for administering 'last rites'. He gave the fish a rap over the head and another for luck. It took several seconds to detach the fish from the fine mesh. When he looked up, Amy was already preparing to cast again.

It was too much. Tony was determined to even the score. "Here!" he said. "My turn." He stepped forward to take the rod just as Amy made her cast. The line slid over his shoulder and the hook caught in his ear. Without thinking, Amy tried to jerk it loose, thereby setting the hook firmly.

It took Tony several seconds to react with a startled howl. By then, Amy had decided that she had done something terrible and that she would be wise to get a long way away. But she was not going to leave her fish behind. Throwing down the rod, she grabbed the slippery fish, scales and slime and blood and all, and, hugging it to her chest, sprinted for home.

Amy expected the direct consequences of her escapade to be dire. She had, after all, committed what she believed was known as Grizzly Bodily Harm on her new friend. But in fact there were no repercussions except that Celandine arrived back at Firhaven in a tizzy because Amy seemed to have vanished, presumably murdered or even kidnapped.

Amy's father returned from the gliding club before the tears were all dried. He chided Amy, firmly but kindly, for abandoning Celandine, congratulated Amy on her fish and lent her several books on trout-fishing, reminders of an earlier passion. Amy, being one of those people who would want to know all about whatever catches their interest, devoured the books even to the point of learning the appearance and uses of many of the flies. If Tony ever came to be on speaking terms with her again, she would at least know about angling. Meanwhile, Celandine made tactful enquiries through her boyfriend and was able to assure the Fergussons that Tony was still alive and well.

But Tony, who had been just as shamed by his own behaviour as Amy was by hers, steered well clear of her for the remaining period of the summer holidays. There was no sign of him at Christmas or Easter nor even when the next summer came round again. Amy, too shy to make direct enquiries, was left to assume that he had been packed off to his mother again in the south of France.

Amy had more to think about that summer than a passing acquaintance. Big changes were in the offing. She and her father each went through mood swings between eagerness and trepidation at the thought of her coming move to boarding school. Mr Fergusson looked forward to having peace and quiet and time to himself but he would miss the company of an enquiring mind and he could imagine Amy returning as a stranger. The house would seem very empty without her. The thought of the school fees also preyed on his mind. Amy, while welcoming escape into a wider and more cosmopolitan world, was haunted by a fear that she would be an outcast among the sophisticates of the BLC and academically far behind them.

In the event, she slotted straight into the largely female, scholastic society. She was far ahead of her contemporaries in maths and science but had some catching up to do in other subjects. She was already almost competent at tennis, but she now learned to play hockey and netball and lacrosse with energy if with no great talent, shone at gymnastics and field events and even played soccer for a junior eleven. She made friends and joined clubs.

When she came home for school holidays and half-term breaks, Mr Fergusson was relieved to find that she was still the same affectionate, helpful and inquisitive Amy but with the addition of a certain poise. He had always allowed her to choose her own clothes, solely because he had not the faintest idea how to go about making a suitable selection. Amy was developing an interest in her own appearance and even a sense of style, choosing, perhaps intuitively, clothes which were suitably girlish yet emphasised the lines of her slender figure. But for most of the time she preferred her old jeans or denim shorts and a sweater or T-shirt. All in all, Mr Fergusson decided, the gamble had been a success.

Two

O n her tenth birthday, Amy received a miniature 35-mil camera. For a while she spent her leisure hours wandering outdoors, watching for interesting flowers or wildlife or people caught off guard.

And then suddenly another summer came round again. By now, she was considered mature enough to be left on her own by day, on the strict understanding that she did not stray beyond the boundaries of home and the adjoining estate. It seemed that Mr Fergusson had met Tony's father, the owner of the Hall, at the gliding club and it had been established that Amy was welcome unless and until she upset Mr Andrews, the head gardener and father of Celandine's beau.

Of this there was little danger. Mr Andrews spent much of his time in the outbuildings and greenhouses, taking cuttings and raising seedlings for his subordinates to plant out and nurture. Amy had first made his acquaintance when her thirst for knowledge had impelled her to ask him the names of some unusual species which she had just photographed. She followed this by asking how cuttings were taken and why they grew roots and why things were pruned only at certain seasons of the year. Mr Andrews was only too pleased to have an appreciative audience and to be photographed performing his magic rites. The outcome was that Amy spent occasional afternoons helping him with the cultivation of rarities. Sometimes she brought cake or jam tarts to go with the many cups of strong tea they took together.

She had almost forgotten the existence of Tony until Mr Andrews one day said, "Master Anthony's home."

"Is he?" Amy had a sudden vision of Tony, still eight years old but grown enormously larger, rampaging after her, seeking revenge for a large hole in his head. She retained her composure and put the picture from her mind.

"M'hm. He was asking if you're still around." Mr Andrews's face took on a roguish look. "Sweet on you, is he?"

"I shouldn't think so," Amy said loftily. "The only time I ever met him, I stuck him with a fish-hook."

Mr Andrews chuckled. "That was you, was it? He came to me to take it out. If he'd gone to any of that lot up at the house, his dad would soon have known all about it and then there'd've been ructions."

"But he didn't?"

"Nah. Valued the skin on his backside too much. Cut the barb off, I did, so that he could take it out himself."

"Did he mind a lot?"

"Him? Not a bit. Boasting about it, he was, to the outdoor staff. To hear him, you'd think he'd been harpooned. Got the two bits in a little frame beside his bed."

Somewhat relieved, Amy set off on her way home. She was carrying a small tray of *gentiana septemfida* seedlings, for Mr Andrews always rewarded her for her help with some of the surplus from his own propagations. Rabbits were out on the grass of the park and a pheasant startled her by rocketing with a great whirring of wings and an angry chortle. The park was looking its summertime best but the reminder of her guilt had quite spoiled her mood.

Where the main drive took a curve between two stands of tall but slender *libocedrus*, the 'Incense Cedar' as Mr Andrews called it, she met Tony. He was tiptoeing along the verge with an obviously home-made bow and arrow, glowering at the rabbits which were staying out of bowshot but otherwise paying him little attention. She could not avoid meeting him without making an ill-mannered detour over the grass. Her first thought as they came closer was that he had shrunk. But she had learned something at her earlier, co-educational school and she realised that she had begun the early spurt of growth to which girls are prone. She was also acutely conscious of her old jeans and black-rimmed fingernails.

As soon as he saw her, Tony discarded his weapons in the handy ditch and beamed. "Hello there!" he said.

"Hello yourself," she said, greatly relieved. "You're not still angry with me?"

"I never was." He sounded quite jovial. "Is that why you rushed away? I needed you to help me take the hook out."

"Mr Andrews said that he had to cut the barb off. Do you have a scar?"

He showed her his ear. "Only a tiny mark. I was going to get a gold ring in it, but Mrs Houston – that's the housekeeper – she wouldn't let me. I told her that I'd caught it on a thorn. It seems a waste of having an ear pierced."

"I suppose I'll have to get my ears pierced some day," Amy said thoughtfully. "Does it hurt?"

Tony hesitated. He seemed to be choosing between boasting of the agonies he had suffered without a murmur of complaint as against dismissing pain as being beneath his notice. "I never felt it," he said at last. "That fish of yours was a ruddy fluke."

From her reading of her father's angling books she realised that, whether or not she knew it at the time, she had done all the right things; but he had been her host and it had been his rod and line, so if he wanted it that way he could have it. "Of course it was," she said. "We'll try again some time and I bet you catch a whopper."

He beamed again. Honour and male pride were satisfied.

"What'll we do?" he asked.

"I can't do anything much. My dad's away gliding again. He's a member of the club."

"So's mine, but he says he never has time to go these days. He's in London today."

"Mine goes to the airstrip every day. He doesn't *fly* every day," Amy explained. "Getting towed up by an aeroplane's too expensive for that, he says, and he has my school fees to pay. I told him that he could save a lot of money by not sending me away to school."

"Did it work?" Tony asked curiously.

"No. So quite often he just goes and helps pushing the gliders around. Sometimes he takes me with him and we both push. You always push a glider backwards, did you know that? It's because the front of the wings is stronger than the back. And sometimes he acts as duty pilot."

"What does the duty pilot do?"

"I don't know exactly, but it seems very important. He's promised to take me up gliding soon."

Tony hid all traces of envy. "I've been up in a helicopter," he said proudly, trumping her ace. "My dad owns one. Or at least it belongs to one of his firms."

That, Amy decided, was what her dad called a conversation-stopper. "I've got to get home now," she told him. "I promised to put dinner on and I'd better get these plants into the ground before they dry out. You can come with me if you like."

"All right." They fell naturally into step. Amy's arms had begun to ache and when she complained he took the tray from her. "How do you like your school?" he asked.

Amy had to think about that. School had simply been one of the facts of life. As part of the natural order of things, school was required to pass judgements on her. It had never occurred to her to judge it in return. "It's pretty good," she decided. "Plenty of games. In some ways it's strict, but not about things I really mind. And sometimes it's boring, having to try to listen to things I'm not interested in. I'd rather be here. When I'm married, I don't think I'll send my children to boarding school."

"Oh yes? And who do you plan to get married to?"

Amy's vague vision of the future had not progressed to far as to identify a possible husband. "I don't know," she said. "I'll think of someone if they don't think of me first."

Tony glanced at her speculatively. "If you go on growing so fast," he said, "you'll end up ten feet tall and nobody wants a wife that big."

"Girls get tall earlier than boys, silly," she said.

They pushed through the gap in the hedge into the garden of Firhaven. Tony wanted to help to plant the gentians in the rockery but Amy decided that he was too neat and clean for gardening in his grey slacks and white shirt. She allowed him to fetch a watering can and fill it from the greenhouse tap.

When the plants were bestowed to her satisfaction and well watered in, Amy led him into the kitchen and switched on the fan oven. She looked up at the wall-clock. "Just in time," she said.

"Are you allowed to cook?"

"I'm learning cookery," she said. "I enjoy it. At least you're never hungry when you're cooking." She was tempted to exaggerate her achievements but decided that one boastful person at a time was quite enough. Tony, she had decided, needed to be kept in his place. "I'm not allowed to fry things unless there's somebody with me. But fried things aren't good for you anyway. And I can only use the back rings on the cooker, just in case. But I'm allowed to make tea and coffee and set the table."

She poured iced lemonade. She looked at the clock again. "Hang on here. I'll be back in a minute."

She dashed up the stairs. She would have liked to take a shower but that would have taken too long. She managed a wash and a change into a light summer dress. She brushed her hair out into its natural waves and decided that that would do.

Downstairs, she looked at the clock again and lit the gas under the potatoes. When she began to lay the table where Tony was sitting, he seemed surprised. "Do you eat here?"

She turned slightly pink. "We have a dining room. But when Dad and I are alone, we eat in here. It's easier."

"I suppose it would be," he said doubtfully.

"It is," she said. "Definitely. Don't you ever eat in the kitchen?"

"No, never. Cook wouldn't like it."

"Really? How is Saint Tropez?"

A shadow came over his usually cheerful face. "Not great. Like you, I'd rather be here."

"I thought there'd be a lot of water-sports and company and . . . and things."

"I can swim here. There's a pool behind the house. You can come and use it if you like. There's a lot of people come to Saint Tropez but most of them are older. And they're a bit stand-offish, too.

"I hate people who are like that, don't you?"

He knew exactly what she meant. "Yes. And I hate people who have no business telling me what to do, but tell me anyway. Who else do you hate?"

She was not a hating sort of person, but she thought about it. "I hate people . . . who show a lot of gum when they smile."

"And I hate people . . . who smell of cheap talcum powder."

"My Dad says he hates people who take a good idea

and do it badly and ruin it so that nobody ever tries it again. Like communism and United Nations and religion and public transport and atomic power, he said."

"That's cheating," Tony said. "I asked you about your hates, not your dad's."

"All right." Amy thought again. When you got into it, the new game was rather fun. "I hate people who pretend to listen but they aren't really listening at all."

"I do, too. And I *really* hate people who think that their time's worth more than mine, so they can keep me waiting while I'd rather be somewhere else doing something different."

"And I hate people who laugh when there's nothing funny."

"And people who do nothing themselves but want to stop other people doing things."

Mr Fergusson came home just in time to prevent the potatoes going to mush. Amy had forgotten to put on the carrots. She and Tony were in deep discussion and fits of giggles.

Two days later, while Amy and her father were working in the garden, Tony arrived at the gap in the hedge. He greeted Mr Fergusson respectfully. "Can Amy come out, Sir? Or is she too busy?"

Mr Fergusson appreciated being called 'Sir' by one of the young generation. He was pleased to smile on Tony. "She's busy, but of course she can go out. She's her own boss in holiday times. A garden should be your haven, not your master. I'm thinking of putting up a sign that says 'This garden is for being happy in, not for working at', except that I can't think of a wording that doesn't have so many terminal prepositions."

Amy, whose English teacher had no hang-ups about the ending of sentences, would not have recognised a terminal preposition if it had bitten her. "You always catch me when I'm filthy," she said.

Tony looked at her critically. "You look fine," he said, attracting a startled look from Mr Fergusson.

Amy accepted the compliment with dignity. "Thank you. But I'm going to clean up anyway. What are we going to do? Fish?"

For a moment, Tony looked pained. "They won't be biting in this weather," he said. "I've got a new bike."

"I've got an old one," Amy said. "It's probably a valuable antique. Hang on a minute while I have a wash."

"Bring a costume," Tony said. "We could have a swim. It's too hot for tennis."

Amy dashed indoors. She seemed always to be performing hasty ablutions in Tony's honour. When she returned, in sandals and shorts over her one-piece bathing suit, carrying a towel and with her camera slung over her shoulder, her father was answering some probing questions about gliding.

"Dad's promised to take me gliding tomorrow," Amy said.

"He was telling me." Tony sighed. "Lucky old you. It looks much more suave than a noisy old helicopter. Come on."

It would have been a long way round by the gates, so Tony helped her to lift her bicycle through the gap in the hedge. Mr Fergusson cast up his eyes. He could see the day coming when the gap would have to be replaced by a proper gate, but it would be worth it. He rather liked young Tony and he had been worried that Amy had lacked company during the holidays. It would be good for her to spend time with Tony.

A smart new boy's bike leaned against a tree on the Hall side of the hedge. In perfect amity, they rode up to the big house and changed to single file to follow a broad path that led around one side. Amy had expected the pool to be marked by a tall fence or hedge for privacy, but there was only a hedged recess to shelter a group of plastic recliners. The large, kidney-shaped pool was set into a slight depression in the garden so that at first glance it seemed almost to be a natural feature. It was only separated from flowering shrubs by a broad, tiled path and a border of rocks. Their arrival caused a momentary flutter among the butterflies clustered on a group of buddleias. The scent of lilac and jasmine hung in the air. The pool itself was new, fresh and filled with sparklingly clean water over blue tiles.

Tony had had the forethought to wear trunks under his shirt and shorts. In a few seconds, the bikes and surplus clothing were deposited with the recliners. The day was a scorcher or, as Amy put it, "There's a huge high got stuck over the Continent and what breeze there is is being drawn up from Spain." The water was cool enough to be invigorating. Amy was a good swimmer but Tony had learned a fast crawl that she was unable to match, which was all that he needed to raise his spirits to the heights. They swam and splashed and dived from a single springboard, photographed each other behaving idiotically and were totally happy with each other's company.

When the chill of the water began to bite, they climbed out into the warm sunshine and towelled themselves, but Tony was still in a competitive mood. "Race you round the pool," he said.

"Running?"

That was what Tony had meant, but on reflection Amy's longer legs might have been a match for his more muscular ones. "On the bikes," he said.

"You're on."

After a few circuits it was clear that Amy could not keep up. They halted, panting, beside the diving board. "Not fair," Amy said lightly. "Your bike's lighter than mine and you've got umpteen gears."

Tony's chin came up. "If that's what you think, let's swap bikes and I'll still beat you."

"Right. Show me how the gears work."

They were more evenly matched now. Tony shot off with Amy, once she had mastered the gears, in close pursuit but unable to pass. The housekeeper, a plump lady of rather more years than she admitted to, hearing screams of laughter, looked out of an upper window, smiled indulgently but told the housemaid that it would end in tears.

On the fourth lap Tony left a gap and Amy saw her chance. She forced more speed and went to overtake on the inside. Tony had no intention of being overtaken by a girl even if he was riding a girl's bike. He crowded across. Amy went into the pool, bike and all.

The mishap seemed hilarious. Their laughter made their dives for the sunken bike more difficult, but they rescued it between them without quite drowning and stood coughing and giggling.

"Best of three?" Amy said. "I start first this time."

"Go!"

Shrieking at the tops of their voices, they circled the pool. Amy guarded the fastest line until, in frustration, Tony tried to force a way past along the edge of the pool. Amy pulled across, determined that Tony should take his turn for a ducking. Tony fought back. The two leaned together, laughing and yelling. Tony was the heavier and he was on the heavier bike. Suddenly, Amy skidded, wobbled and crashed. She landed on her back on the tiles and stayed there.

Tony was horrified. He dropped the other bike into a bed of heathers and ran back. "Amy! Are you all right?"

"I think so. I feel a little bit sick." She was very white. She put out a hand and Tony pulled her to her feet. "My other arm hurts."

Tony turned her round. "You've cut your elbow on one of the stones," he said. There was a lot of blood, but he was afraid to tell her that. "You'd better come into the house. Quickly."

Amy tried to look at her elbow. She managed to see it over her shoulder by putting her arm back. Bone was showing white and blood was trickling down to her fingers. She was beginning to feel dizzy and Tony's voice seemed to echo. "Yes," she said faintly. "Is your bike all right?"

"Never mind my damn bike. Come *on*."

She started to walk towards the house but there was

a great hissing in her ears and the sunlight became night-time.

Tony caught her before she fell. She was very light but she had no convenient handles to get hold of and he might never have been able to lift her limp body if she had reached the ground again. He hurried with her towards the house, calling for help.

Amy, though fuddled by loss of blood, was vaguely aware of being taped up by Mr Hope-Williams's housekeeper and then removed by ambulance the twenty miles to the local hospital. When she came fully back to her senses, she was in a hospital bed with a cast on one arm and a drip in the other.

Her father was by her bedside. "It wasn't Tony's fault," she said quickly.

"Of course not," said Mr Fergusson. "Young people fall off bikes all the time, but they don't usually do themselves quite so much damage or give their poor old parents such a scare. You do have a helmet, you know."

"I do know that. But we were only riding around the pool. I'd have looked absolutely daft in a swimsuit and crash helmet. Anyway, the helmet wouldn't have saved my elbow."

"When did you ever worry about what you looked like? Young Tony's outside. He asks after you every ten minutes on the dot. You have a conquest there."

Amy guessed that he was only trying to hide his anxiety and cheer them both up. Even so this was going Over The Top – there were five other beds in the ward but nobody seemed to be paying them any attention.

However, she said, "Please don't be funny about it, Dad."

Mr Fergusson winked. "All right. So it's a sensitive subject. But if you ever come to think about a rich husband, he'll be available and probably willing. I've had a chat with the doctor or house surgeon or whatever he calls himself. As well as gashing your elbow on a flint and losing a lot of blood, you've managed to chip the bone. They've removed the chip and sewn up your arm, but they want to keep you for twenty-four hours or so to replace the lost blood, make sure that you're over the shock and to put on a permanent cast."

"Permanent?"

"Not that sort of permanent, Juggins. But the one you have on is temporary for now. They'll replace it when they've had another look and they'll take it off again to remove your stitches. I'm afraid you're going to have a sore arm for a few weeks."

The awful meaning behind his words suddenly struck her. "Dad! If I stay in here for twenty-four hours, I'll miss my going up in the glider!"

He sighed and took her hand. "I'm sorry. I know you've been looking forward to it. But I couldn't possibly take you up with your arm like that. I was going to ask you . . . I told the club secretary to write my name against the two-seater on the flying list first thing tomorrow, so I'll have to pay the club for the glider anyway. Would you mind terribly if I took Tony up instead? He hasn't said so aloud but I can see that he's very keen to go."

She was glad that she was on her back. If she had been sitting up, she thought that the tears would have run down her face. It was so unfair. Tony, the one who had almost hurled her in among the rocks, the person who had already had a flight in a helicopter and didn't *need* to go gliding, was going to have *her* turn and be taken up by *her* father. And she couldn't object without seeming a real dog in the manger. Life was a turd in aspic, somebody had said, and now she saw that it was a perfect description.

"I suppose you may as well," she said. "But, Dad, can you fix it again for later?"

"Yes, of course I can," he said. "But it won't be during these holidays."

"Dad!"

"I'm sorry. I've been looking forward to it as much as you have. It's time that we developed some common interests and did more things together. While you were a little girl, I never quite knew what to talk to you about. Nowadays, we mostly talk about meteorology.

"But think about it. You'll have a tender arm and a stiff one at that. Suppose we hit a patch of turbulent air or had to make a rough landing. Suppose, even, that there was a mid-air collision and we had to use parachutes . . ."

She tried to sit up but found that she didn't have the strength. "Does that happen?"

He was grateful for the chance to rub a little of the icing off the cake. "Gliders do sometimes collide if somebody forgets the rule of the air, though they usually seem to land safely. My guess is that we average about six bale-outs a year in Britain. It's not exactly a rule that we wear parachutes, except for aerobatics; but it's an almost universal habit, so general opinion must be that

30

there could come a time when we'll need them. It can get a bit crowded in a good thermal."

"You'll be sure to tell Tony that?"

"I expect so. Why?"

"I don't mind him having my flight as long as he doesn't enjoy it."

He laughed, not least because she had reminded him of a rude story which she was still far too young to hear. "I can understand that," he said, "even if I can't really approve. I'll arrange your flight again as soon as I can."

"Christmas?"

"You know there's very little gliding at Christmas. The weather can be dodgy and people have other things on their minds – like the danger of a collision with Santa's sleigh."

Amy threw her eyes in the direction which would normally have been up. On this occasion it afforded her only a view of the black metal bed-head and the stand for the drip. "Dad, really!"

"Sorry. I know you're a big girl now, I'm just sorry that you're growing up so quickly. But your flight will have to be Easter or next summer. Now, do you feel strong enough to endure a visit from Tony?"

"I suppose. Do I look all right?"

"He will undoubtedly think so."

"Dad, you're doing it again! Anyone would think that you're in a hurry to have to pay for a fancy wedding with all the trimmings."

Mr Fergusson smiled complacently. "I've started an insurance policy," he said. He left the small ward. Amy, not ill pleased by his last compliment, touched her hair, but it seemed to be reasonably tidy. She lay back and assumed what she guessed would be a suitably wan and fragile appearance.

Tony came in, very gingerly, and perched on the one chair. "How are you doing?" he asked in a whisper.

"I'll be all right," she whispered back.

"I'm sorry," he said. "So sorry. It was all my fault."

She forgot about maintaining the semblance of an invalid. "It wasn't anything of the sort," she said firmly. "We should both have known better, racing around on slippery tiles and no helmets or anything. Anyway, I asked for it. You paid me back for sticking a Butcher in your ear."

He grabbed for her hand. She saw that he was trying not to cry and she looked away. "I'm so glad. You're my very best friend and I wouldn't want that spoiled. And you don't mind . . . Did your dad tell you . . . ?"

"That you're going up in the glider instead of me? Yes, I do mind, but it isn't your fault and there's nothing either of us can do about it."

His grip on her hand tightened. "I won't go if you don't want me to."

"That would be silly," she said. She felt rather noble, as if she had offered herself for sacrifice for the sake of the others, whoever they might be. "The glider's organised and it'll have to be paid for. There'd be no point not using it just so as not to hurt my feelings. You may as well go. You can tell me all about it afterwards."

"I'll do that." He smiled for a moment and then looked solemn again. "It's a shame that you had to fall off just when we were having such a good afternoon."

She sighed. She decided not to quibble about his version of her accident. "It was good, wasn't it?"

"The best I ever had."

"Me too." Looking back, she suddenly realised that she could not remember a better.

"Would you like me to bring you some books?"

"I suppose so, if I'm going to be stuck at home for a while. I won't be riding my bike for yonks. Hey, is my bike all right?"

"It's OK. I'll clean the rust off and give it an oil and bring it down to you."

"Thanks. And your bike?"

"The handlebars were squint but I've straightened them. It's lost a little paint. Nothing that a touch-up kit won't fix."

"That's all right, then," Amy said. She searched her mind for another topic of conversation. It was hard work being visited in hospital. "Do you have a lot of books?"

He looked more animated. "Tons," he said. "I like reading and books are something my dad doesn't mind paying for. Reading's much better than just seeing things on the telly. You can read it in your own time, skip bits, go back to re-read anything that you enjoyed or didn't quite understand first time through and put your own choice of faces to the characters. It must be marvellous to be able to tell a story like that and have everybody read it. I'm going to be a writer someday."

"Doesn't your dad want you to follow him into the business?"

"Yes." Tony frowned ferociously as he struggled to

verbalise his innermost thoughts. "I'd rather he gave me an allowance and just let me write, but I suppose I'll have to go along with him. I'm not bad at money things and somebody told me that most writers have a job as well, at least until they get going."

When Mr Fergusson returned, they were arguing heatedly over the relative merits of different authors.

The following afternoon, Amy was judged to be sufficiently recovered to go and recuperate at home and leave the hospital bed for somebody more in need of it. When her father came for her, she was wheel-chaired down to the front entrance and helped carefully into the car. It looked like a perfect gliding afternoon. There had been thunder in the night and the day was clear and cool with a moderate breeze and signs of lenticular clouds near the distant hills. As they drove off she said in a disinterested voice, "Did you go up?"

"Yes."

"With Tony?"

"Yes."

"How did he do?"

Mr Fergusson was concentrating on his entry into the traffic flow outside the hospital gates. "H'm?" he said. Amy repeated her question. When they were out on the main road, he said, "He was too nervous to do anything at first. A common reaction. When he'd settled down a bit and came to believe that the wings weren't going to fall off any second, he followed me through the control inputs."

"Did he fly the glider himself?" Amy asked.

"Only straight and level. I cut it short after that. It seemed to be quite enough of an experience for one day."

"More than enough," Amy said.

Three

Amy was glad to get to her bed early that evening. The hospital had provided her with painkillers which were doled out sparingly by her father, but for the second night running the difficulty of finding a comfortable position with one arm in a cast delayed the onset of sleep. She called up a mental picture of fishing a deep and placid pool and as always the relaxing image worked its magic. Once she had managed to drop off, she slept as only the young can sleep. The pain in her arm woke her, but she awoke refreshed and after a late and hearty breakfast, thanks largely to the recuperative powers of youth, she had recovered most of her strength.

Any idea that she might go dashing up to the Hall was firmly put down. Her father had already garnered the overnight data from the Air Ministry and other sources and run his computer programs and now, between coping with most of the housework and exchanging faxes with a multitude of clients, was also acting as her nurse and keeper. She offered to help, in any capacity, but all offers were refused on the grounds that she was an invalid. Privately, he reflected that being helped would undoubtedly take him longer than working alone.

So Amy was established in a deck chair in a corner of the garden well sheltered from the wind while her father blasted his way through the manifold tasks. She was sitting peacefully there in mid-morning. She had read everything she could find about trout and salmon fishing and now considered herself to be tolerably expert. Now she had moved onward to reading one of her father's gliding manuals – because learning about something, she had found, was almost as much fun as doing it – when she was interrupted.

"You have visitors," said her father's voice. "Messrs Hope-Williams, Senior and Junior."

Rightly interpreting this to mean Tony and his father, Amy glanced at the gap in the hedge, but they emerged from the French windows. Mr Fergusson brought more deck chairs. "Would anyone like coffee?"

"Thanks for the offer, but we've just had breakfast," said Tony's father – rather impatiently, Amy thought. He settled himself carefully in one of the deck chairs, testing its strength and stability. Tony and Amy shook their heads.

"Then I'll leave you to it and get on with earning a living," Mr Fergusson said, making his escape.

Mr Hope-Williams was an imposing man, tall, red-faced and red-haired, heavily built and deep-chested, stern-looking and with a loud and authoritative voice. Superficially he seemed totally unlike Tony and yet Amy could detect a resemblance in the shape of their skulls, the profiles of their noses and jaws and occasionally in the timbre of their voices. Amy had seen Tony's father in the distance, speaking to Mr Andrews or being swept along one of the drives in a glossy, chauffeur-driven car, but had never before heard his voice. His accent was not quite as perfect as that of a BBC newsreader but a passable imitation. Amy, who had thought of fathers as benevolent if sometimes woolly-minded providers, began to understand why Tony's voice had always dipped respectfully when he mentioned his father.

"Now, young lady," he said. "So you're the person who bled all over my tiles."

Amy felt a stab of guilt. "I'm sorry," she said. "Shall I come and clean it up?"

Mr Hope-Williams stared at her in astonishment. "Lord, no! It was a joke. I have staff for that sort of thing. Tell me, how did it happen?"

Out of the corner of her eye, Amy saw Tony stiffen. She was usually truthful, but Tony was her friend. "It was my fault," she said. "I was riding my bike and I fell off. I think I skidded on a place where we'd splashed water. I came down on my back and hit my elbow on a stone."

Tony began to breathe again.

"And this young man wasn't to blame?"

"Not the least bit. And he was very helpful afterwards."

For the first time, Mr Hope-Williams's face relaxed and even showed the faintest shadow of a smile. "That's all right, then. Your father's a good man. I subscribe to his forecasting service and we've met at the gliding club. I wouldn't want to lose his goodwill. I'll leave you now to recuperate in peace. You can have young Anthony for company."

With that generous gesture, and without having made

the customary enquiry as to how she was feeling, Mr Hope-Williams rose, nodded and walked away. Listening, Amy just managed to hear a car drift quietly away from the front of the house.

"Phew!" she said, lacking words.

Tony nodded. "He says he's grooming me to take over all his businesses when he retires," he said gloomily.

"You'll be rich," Amy pointed out. "Aren't you pleased?"

"Not if it's going to make me get like him, ordering people around and getting ulcers. I'd rather be a writer. Or anything. Thanks for not dropping me in it."

"What are friends for?" Amy asked. "Is that why he came? To find out if you'd knocked me off my bike?"

Tony giggled – there was no other word for it. "I think he came mostly to see if you were suitable company for me and not the sort of girl who'd lead me astray."

"I must have passed the test or he wouldn't have left you here for me to teach you rude words and bad habits. How did the gliding go?" Amy asked.

Tony brightened immediately and then looked worried. "What would you like me to say?"

Amy understood immediately. "I'd like the absolute truth," she said. "No white lies between us, ever."

"All right, then. It was great! Not like a helicopter at all. Quiet and floaty. We went up behind a small plane. When we were miles and miles high, your dad pulled a lever that dropped the tow-line and he brought us over here and I looked down. You wouldn't believe what big roofs the Hall has. Then he let me take the stick and I flew around for ages. He said that I did very well."

Of the two versions, Amy was more inclined to believe

her father's but she decided to give Tony the benefit of the doubt. "Wow!" she said. It seemed to be expected.

"But of course I didn't know about thermals and things and when we began to run out of height it was time to come in. Your dad took over control and landed on the airstrip, but it wasn't anything I couldn't have done. I've asked my father if I can take gliding lessons whenever I'm here."

"What did he say?"

Tony flushed. "The sort of thing some parents always say. He said to wait until I'm older and that I've got to stick to my schoolbooks. I know he's my father, and he must have been a boy himself back in the age of the dinosaurs, but he just doesn't understand. We just don't seem to be living in the same world."

"Huh!" Amy snorted. "You think that you're the only one with a problem? My dad never was a girl. But he does try, I think."

"Mine doesn't," Tony said. "Not in that sense. He's caught up in making another million or two and I'm just a nuisance underfoot, like a cowpat or something."

Amy was finding Tony's lack of filial loyalty slightly shocking. "I don't think that you should say things like that. Not to a stranger, anyway."

"But you're not a stranger. How would you like to swap dads?"

Amy considered the hypothesis seriously. "I'd rather not, if you don't mind," she said at last.

"There you are, then. I just wish he was different, more like yours."

"If you feel like that, I'm surprised that you come

here to the Hall. Why don't you go to your mother?"

"That's worse in a different sort of way. Dad says he's grooming me for business, but I'm sure he thinks I'll never be any good at it. Mum keeps thinking up new careers she thinks I'd be marvellous at. I don't know which is worse, really. But I don't have much choice – they send me to and fro like a tennis ball." He made a face. "Anyway, I'd much rather be here. Let's talk about something else."

"All right." Amy cast about for a topic that might restore his flagging ego. "They said that when I fainted you carried me into the house. Is that what happened?"

"Just about."

"Well, I think that's very romantic," Amy said. "Just like in a film or a book."

"Rubbish!" Tony said, but he looked gratified. "In a sort of way, I suppose you could think that. I brought you some books to read." He took several volumes out of a carrier-bag and put them on the table, retaining one. "This is my favourite," he said. "Don't lose it or put coffee-cups down on it or anything. It's autographed. Dad got it for me. That's one time he got a present right. I think this man's books are great. It must be wonderful to be able to tell a story like that."

Amy took the book from him. *Unsafe Haven*, it said. The author's name was repeated in a flamboyant scrawl on the fly-leaf. "Derek Cardinal," she said. "I've heard of him and I think I've seen him on the telly." She flipped to the back of the dust-jacket and studied the photograph. "That's him. He was being interviewed on a chat show. Something about another of his books being made into a film. I liked him, a rather sweet old man with a nice smile and a gentle sense of humour. Does your dad know him?"

"He knows everybody. But Mr Cardinal lives near here and he's a member of the gliding club. He's been to dinner at the Hall, but not," Tony said regretfully, "while I was at home."

"I'll read it this afternoon and tell you what I think tomorrow," Amy promised.

For the rest of that summer, they were constant companions. At first, while Amy was wearing her cast, swimming and cycling were impractical. Amy devoured *Unsafe Haven*. Her previous ventures into adult reading had been confined to school-subject classics, which she had found heavygoing, and some rather patronising works aimed at the young adult market which quite failed to hold her attention. But the books of Derek Cardinal opened a new world to her. Her father had another of Cardinal's books on his shelf and Tony was able to lend her two more. The stories gripped her with excitement. They were told in lucid English, but with sudden outbursts of humour and with imagery which brought reality to each scene. The characters were so whole that she would have recognised any of them, Amy thought, if she had met them in the street. Threaded through the stories were love-themes which, though beyond Amy's immediate comprehension, made her feel that some day she might be glad to be a woman. She found that she could read each book over and over, gaining fresh insight with every reading.

There was more to their companionship than forming a Derek Cardinal Fan Club. Once Tony was assured that the encumbrance on her arm would prevent Amy from casting a fly-line, she was privileged to accompany Tony and to watch his pursuit of the trout. She managed, using her utmost tact, to convey some of the lore which she had gleaned from her father's books plus the wisdom which the bystander often gains simply by standing back and watching, so that Tony's casting improved to the point at which he was regularly catching fish. Soon he was quoting back to her as his own some of the knowledge that she had conveyed to him.

But Amy's cast was removed at last and the weather, after an interval of drizzle, returned to what summer should be. As her elbow slowly mended, they cycled together, confining their occasional races to the grass, and they swam and lazed in the sun or the shade as the whim took them. They discussed the world's problems and solved them all to their own satisfaction.

"When I'm Prime Minister," Amy said suddenly one day, "I'll pass a law making parents responsible for any damage done by their children. And if a child commits a crime, the parent can go to jail for it." There had been some petty vandalism in the village and the villagers were up in arms.

"Going into politics now, are we?" said Tony lazily. They were lying on their backs under a huge chestnut tree, looking up through the branches towards glimpses of a sharply blue sky. "You'll have the civil-rights people at your throat."

43

"But I'll also have a generation of well-behaved children becoming well-behaved grown-ups," Amy retorted. "Of course, civic responsibility would have to become part of the school curriculum."

"You'd have to lift a lot of the restrictions on the police," Tony said. His father had been thundering on the subject. "Give them a fair chance to catch the offender and get a conviction."

"Good idea! What a pity term-time's almost round again. At Christmas, let's start a list of all the new laws there ought to be and all the old ones that should be scrapped. Then we can go and shout at the candidates next time an election comes round."

"I like it," Tony said. "I definitely like it."

By the time that he pushed through the gap in the hedge next morning, Amy had thought some more. "We'll have to do away with all this anonymity for offenders," she said. "My dad says that prisons are just universities of crime. Naming and shaming, that's what we want. Public apologies and community service. I think I'll bring back the stocks and the pillory. Tony, what's wrong?"

Tony flopped onto the other garden chair. He was looking thoroughly fed up. "I don't think I'll be here at Christmas," he said. "You'll have my vote when I'm old enough, but you'll have to prepare your whajacallit, your manifesto, on your own. My dad's been bringing women here at the weekends. He tells me that they're his secretary or a typist, but I know his secretary's voice and I usually hear the stairs creak in the night, so I don't think it's business. And now he's going to marry one of them. What does he want to do a thing like that for?"

The question almost stumped Amy. "Perhaps he wants somebody to look after him," she suggested.

"He's got a whole lot of staff to look after him," Tony said peevishly. "And he wants me to be his best man, which means dressing up and making a speech and things, but he says he'll write the speech for me. Well, at least it'll get me a break from school. But he doesn't want me around the house so much when he's married. I make the place look untidy or something. She already has kids of her own and they're pretty awful. I'll be spending most of my holidays in Saint Tropez, I suppose."

Privately, Amy could think of worse fates than being banished to the south of France with its film stars and sunshine, but Tony seemed to be dreading the prospect. "Maybe you can get gliding lessons there," she suggested.

Tony shook his head violently. "Mum's worse than Dad. Won't let me do anything at all in case I damage myself. I can't even swim except where there's a life-guard. Mind you, the Med's an absolute sewer. I wouldn't let any kid of mine swim in it."

"You wouldn't be able to do a lot here when there's a step mother and family in residence," Amy suggested.

But Tony was not to be comforted. "I don't suppose they'll even be here most of the time. They don't seem to be country sort of people. I don't want to go away. I don't want to lose touch with you."

"Me?"

"You're my friend. My *best* friend. When I go, let's write to each other and send photographs and things."

"All right," Amy said. "I'll miss you too. It's been fun having you next door."

45

"Really?" Tony actually blushed. "I'm glad. And listen. There's a spare key to the fishing-hut. I'll give it to you and a letter and things to say that it's all right for you to fish there as my guest while I'm away, if you promise to write and tell me what you catch and on what fly."

Amy was touched by this evidence of thoughtfulness on the part of the usually selfish Tony. "Thanks," she said. "I'll do that. But we still have a few days. Let's make the most of them. What'll we do?"

Tony thought for only a moment. "Let's go and build a tree-house," he said.

"Good thinking," said Amy. "But make it somewhere I can climb to without bending my arm more than a bit."

The school holidays, as usual, ended much too soon, just when Amy's elbow was returning almost to its previous mobility. As he feared, Tony was condemned to spend most of the succeeding holidays with his mother.

The two friends exchanged Christmas cards and presents by post but Amy could not buy, during the British winter, anything for Tony to take to the beach in the south of France, while Tony, on the Riviera, was stumped for anything that Amy could wear in the snow and sleet which had taken over in Britain. In desperation, she sent him cuff-links and he sent her clip-on earrings, and each was delighted.

It was not until Easter that they met again. In March, Tony's father had married the Hon. Felicia Mount with Tony as best man and, when the apparently happy couple went on honeymoon to St Lucia, Tony was allowed to remain at the Hall. He and Amy were each aware of a glow of contentment at seeing the other again although they were too young to say so without embarrassment. Tony had become again definitely the taller of the two.

The weather was not in their favour. "It's too cold to swim," Tony said gloomily, "and in the summer I'll be back in Saint Tropez where it'll be too hot to do anything." They were stretched out on the hearth-rug before a log fire in the drawing room of the Hall with an abandoned chess game in front of them.

"Never mind," Amy said. "There's always school."

"You like school?" Surprise was evident in Tony's voice.

"I don't mind it. A lot of the stuff's interesting, some of it's quite fun and there's plenty of company. You never have to kick your heels, wondering what to do next."

"I suppose that's so. But we never have to do that when we're here."

"It can get a bit boring here when you're with your mum." Amy looked at him searchingly. "You sound as if you're unhappy at school?"

Tony considered. "That would be putting it a bit strong. Sometimes it's all right," he said. "I just don't like being bossed around and regimented and made to feel that I'm a useless little nobody at the bottom of the heap. Don't you feel that you'd like to get away on your own sometimes, be yourself and do your own thing?"

"Not very often," Amy said. "Do you?"

"Now and again. I mean quite often, really. When I've had enough of people and being chased around, I imagine myself shut away privately in a study, writing away like nobody's business, or up in a glider on my own, in a silent world high above the clouds, looking down on the earth and everybody bustling around and annoying each other miles below. Has your dad taken you up yet?"

Amy accepted that a change of subject was due. "I'd have written and told you if he had. The weather's been too awful. Well, look at it!"

Tony looked. The world outside was shrouded in mist and dripped drizzle. "It's funny to think that the sun will be shining up above," he said.

Amy made a farting noise with her mouth. "Well, it isn't shining down here and down here's where we'd have to land and take off. Dad's been promising to take me up as soon as we get the weather, provided he's free that day."

"You'll probably enjoy it. You'll just have to remember that there's nothing to be afraid of. Is he going to give you lessons?"

Amy felt a moment of irritation. She could stand being patronised by her elders and betters but Tony, although he had a year's advantage, suffered the handicap of being insulated from the world by family wealth and so was often her inferior when it came to worldly wisdom. She kept her reply calm. "He says not. He isn't a qualified instructor, so the rules don't allow him to do more than take somebody up and give them a gentle introduction. So I asked when I could get lessons and he's too kind to say out loud, 'Not for a long time – now go away and stop bugging me,' but that was what he meant. I asked why and he said that I was still too small for the parachute harness, but I don't think that that's right."

"It could be because of the cost," Tony suggested. Despite his father's affluence, he was developing an almost intuitive understanding of the value of money and people's attitudes to it.

"It can't be that," Amy said. "Lessons are free, because I asked the club secretary and he said that the whole organisation is based on amateurism and the instructors mostly do it because it gets them a lot of free gliding."

"I spoke to the club secretary too. I wanted to be sure that I knew what I was talking about before tackling my dad again. Lessons may be free," Tony said, "but every aerotow launch costs you. And a lesson means a two-seater and a two-seater means a club glider and the club gliders are charged by the *minute*, would you believe? You'll have to try him again when he's feeling rich. Catch him when he's just banked a big cheque. That sometimes works for me, but my Dad still thinks of me as five years old and overjoyed to get a pound now and again."

Amy sighed. "I suppose so. But it's so tedious. Waiting, I mean, for life, real life, to begin."

"I know what you mean. I don't mind the summer term so much," Tony said. "Cricket's not bad. You can be yourself at cricket. Your score may count for the team, but whatever you do you do as yourself. And there's always tennis and squash. It's the winter I hate most. Rugger and soccer and a lot of cold, wet team games that are supposed to toughen you up and teach you to play up, play up and play the game. Toughen you up for what, for Heaven's sake?"

"Dad says that the bodies we build now have to last us the rest of our lives," Amy said, "which I would have thought went without saying. When I'm Queen, I'll let it be known that We do not approve of compulsory PE."

Tony rolled over and sat up. "Queen is it now? Which of the royals are you setting your cap at?"

"I didn't say queen of which country," Amy pointed out.

"No, you didn't." Tony lay back, dislodging the chess pieces. "I don't mind this fitness lark while we're young enough to take it, but I do think there should be a time limit. All these middle-aged men going to gyms and playing squash and having heart attacks. I've seen Dad's friends. Most of them are dead now and no wonder. Can't you just imagine some health freak arriving at the pearly gates and St Peter saying, 'Well, what have you done with your life?' And all he could say would be, 'I've always kept myself fit.'"

"And St Peter would just look at him with one eyebrow up," Amy said.

The pair rolled around on the hearth-rug, chortling.

At the end of the Easter break the pair parted, vowing eternal friendship. They wrote at least once a month, the exchange usually triggered by a letter from Tony. Neither was much inclined towards lengthy and grammatical writing, so they developed and shared a terse, telegraphic style of communication.

Amy wrote in her neat, round script:

At last, my flight, yesterday. Bright day, very calm. Dad got the side-by-side glider, not the tandem, which made things easier. Serious talk about how to use the parachute, enough to make anyone nervous. The cable from the tow-plane was hooked on and before I knew it, up, up and away. Took some photos, copies enclosed.

Before I was ready, Dad suddenly said, 'You have control.' He kept hand lightly on the control thingy. I'd been reading his gliding books, didn't do anything too daft. Just matter of remembering turn as much by banking as rudder while pulling gently back on stick. After a bit it becomes instinctive and you just *think* it round. A glider can only go generally downhill – expect you know all this – and day was too calm so I headed for the industrial estate. He said 'Where do you think you're going?' I said 'Looking for a thermal,' and he said 'Good God!' Sure enough, column of warm air rising from roofs and tarmac. Ground getting smaller and smaller. Dad took control back and went round and round in the thermal. Stayed up for ages, looking down on birds. Dad said that I was grinning right over the top of my head and down my back. Loved it, loved it, loved it! Can't wait to go again.

To which Tony replied in his unformed scrawl:

Great feeling, no? Must be great being a bird, can't understand why they always look so fed up. Have to get your dad to take us again or persuade mine stump up for flying time and launch, for getting instruction. Don't know when get back, though. Hon. Felicia prefers Town, Hall closed with skeleton staff. Don't see why I can't stay there anyway. Wouldn't be in anybody's way. I'll keep working on it.

Your photos were good, brought it all back.

Several letters later, Amy wrote:

Hall gardens being kept up, still go help Mr Andrews sometimes, but not the same – not much more than maintenance, no point propagating annuals when family not there. Just as well they're never here, perhaps – Hon. Felicia not much loved, tried to lord it like your mum did, do the Lady Bountiful bit. Lot of left-wingers here. Now there's a joke going round I'm not supposed to hear about being a better Mount than her mother, which don't understand. Maybe you can explain. Isn't a Mount now anyway, she's a Hope-Williams like you. No, not like you but you know what I mean. Tree house blew down in recent gale. Miss you.

P.S. You were right (for once). Your step-siblings are just what you called them but somebody seems to have told them that money makes up for manners. Not true. Hardly ever at Hall but tried to get me kept off the lake. Showed your dad your letter and he put foot down. Now I can fish and they can't. Caught a two-and-a-half-pounder last week, nearly pulled me into water. A.

Tony by now had acquired a laptop computer. He wrote, and printed in a very fancy fount:

Miss you too and more, but good times will come again some day. I'll explain that joke when you're older.

Four

It was to be several years before they met again but, despite the fickleness of the young, their friendship survived. Their correspondence continued sporadically, becoming rarer when things went well, but almost daily when either was troubled.

Tony moved on to his father's old public school.

Damn! he wrote (or typed). Spent years getting to be a senior, now gone straight from being one of top dogs to new boy, lowest of low. Small frog in huge puddle. Suppose same when university, perhaps all through life. Dad wants me go London School of Economics, follow in his footsteps. Not sure if my scene but should be OK. Maybe it's what I'd do least worst.

Amy wrote back:

Dad wants me to go to proper uni, not LSE; take science, view to following into meteorology. Doesn't sound too bad, fundamental for gliding and nobody expects you to be right all the time. My maths OK. Dad says women have less sense of space than men, unusual to find a female who can visualise wedges of air sliding over each other, but all seems perfectly logical to me. Been gliding once more; Dad seems reluctant – do women bring bad luck in gliders, like in ships?

But the fact was that Mr Fergusson, faced with the increasing drain of school fees, was feeling the pinch. He had his own, not very new glider, which he maintained himself with Amy's help, and he flew it whenever he felt himself to be in sufficient funds, but taking Amy up meant paying for one of the club gliders on top of the significant cost of an aerotow launch. So Amy flew four or five times a year, read everything about gliding that she could put her hands on and dreamed dreams. Perhaps if she had experienced the joy of gliding more often, the magic would have worn off. Youthful enthusiasm is easily sated and sometimes deprivation can turn out to be a blessing, heavily disguised.

Amy progressed to the senior school. She wrote:

This is OK. You're expected to study for yourself instead of being spoon-fed but science and maths come easy. They'd think me a total swot except I'm dynamite at hockey. Easy way out of those compulsory sports you hate so much. Got sent off yesterday – sent the ball mostway down field at head height, leaving vapour trail and making low humming sound, other players throwing selves flat.

Joined dancing club. Boys from nearby schools come in as partners, strictly chaperoned. Taking

evening class in theory and maintenance of cars –
no lady drivers allowed to leave here.

Tony wrote:

My maths is OK but struggling with languages,
except French of course.

The following Easter, Tony's mother was to visit a cousin
in Thailand and his father preferred not to have him
underfoot in London. Tony seized his chance to spend
the break with the skeleton staff at the Hall. To his dismay,
Amy had chosen that period to stay with a schoolfriend in
Yorkshire. Tony wrote:

Wanted to surprise you. Would have been great.
Hall still mostly shut, sort of camping out. Mooched
around. Fished a bit, caught three trout. You left the
flies in a muddle but I've sorted them out. Your
dad took pity, took me up once, let me go round
in a thermal. Mr Andrews's Suzuki failed MOT, he
was going to scrap it but he would have had to pay
someone to take it away. It runs, so I begged it off
him and tried driving it. Legal on private drives. Went
into the bushes once when mind went blank but now
managing OK. Next time I can swing a visit, you
teach me dancing and I'll teach you to drive.

Amy wrote:

Don't like surprises, next time warn me and I'll be

sure to be there. Yes, could have been great and I'd have given up boring Yorkshire to be there. Still miss you.

That Christmas, Tony wrote:

Thanks for photos. You're turning into a lovely piece of crumpet. May see you again sooner than we thought. Mum marrying again, acting like a kid, won't want me around to remind new husband she's older than he is.

Amy wrote back immediately:

Don't ever call me a piece of crumpet or I'll never speak to you again. I'm me and don't you forget it. Glad you approve all the same. Getting hair styled next week. Dad says why don't you come to us for holidays? He wasn't too keen on another mouth to feed – self-employment isn't all it's cracked up to be – but what about a sort of PG? Pay for your food? Try it on.

Tony put the proposition to his parents, telling each that the other was in favour, and the idea was felt to be ideal, leaving each parent free for uninterrupted life with the new family. Tony would be back where he was happy and where he would ultimately reign and he could be invited to join either parent and step-relatives for carefully regulated periods on special occasions.

So they were together again that summer. Amy and

her father met Tony at the station. By then, they found, he was even taller than before and had grown into a rather gangling but attractive youth with curly hair and a sensitive, bony face. Soon, it was as though they had never been apart. They fished, loafed and drove around the estate roads in Mr Andrews's battered old Suzuki (christened, unimaginatively, Suzie) and Amy, fortified by her evening class, earned Tony's great admiration by showing him how to cure a nasty fit of misfiring. When Tony found that he could put his hand on the cellar keys, they made tentative experiments with Mr Hope-Williams's wines and spirits. With Mr Fergusson to operate the hi-fi and act as critic and adjudicator, and with the aid of a popular textbook, Amy passed on her slender understanding of The Dance and they made onward progress together.

Mr Hope-Williams was waking up to the fact that he now had a nearly adult son and he passed on and supplemented the saving on Tony's flights to the Riviera and subsistence while there. Tony's life-style while with the Fergussons made no demands for extravagance other than an occasional visit to the local cinema. When posters went up, advertising a marquee dance at the local fete, he was suddenly inspired. "Let's go and show them how it's done," he said. "It's my treat."

Amy asked around, to be quite sure that she would be dressed neither too 'up' nor too 'down' and the pair enjoyed their evening. Despite his youth, Tony even managed to obtain drinks for them at the crowded bar and when space on the floor permitted their proficiency at line-dancing was widely admired. They walked home, arm-in-arm, through a perfect evening scented with summer blossoms. For all those reasons, Tony may have been slightly above himself when they arrived back at the front door of Firhaven.

He produced the front door key with which he had been entrusted but paused. "Have you enjoyed yourself?" he asked.

"Daft question!" Amy said. "You know I have. It's been a lovely evening."

"Do I deserve a kiss?" he asked in a voice choked with shyness.

Amy hesitated. This was the first time that the difference between their genders had been acknowledged so openly. She gave him a quick peck on the cheek.

"We could do a little better than that," Tony said. He put an arm round her shoulders, but very loosely.

Amy let it remain there but lowered her head. "We could," she said, "but I don't think it would be a very good idea."

"Why not?"

Amy might have lacked personal experience but she had listened and learned. "Because once we start that sort of thing I'd have to draw a line somewhere and say, 'Thus far and no further,' and I don't like drawing lines and you wouldn't like it either. I don't want to hurt your feelings."

"Go ahead and hurt them," Tony said hopefully. "When I go back to school, I'd like to be able to say that at least I'd kissed a girl."

"You could say it anyway," Amy pointed out.

"But, if it wasn't true, I couldn't say it with conviction."

Tony lowered his voice. "Most boys my age have gone all the way."

"Or say they have." In the near darkness, he could not see that she was holding back a grin. "You can go back to school and tell them that you've gone all the way with me if you like. I won't mind. In fact, it might do my social life a whole lot of good."

Tony shied away from the implications. "Just one on the lips."

"Promise me you won't turn back into a frog?"

Tony spluttered with laughter. "That's one promise that I can make and be almost sure of keeping."

"Just one, then. But no tongues, mind." They kissed – a single kiss without tongues. The kiss went on for rather a long time. Perhaps they were waiting to see whether Tony would turn back into a frog, but he kept his promise. They parted at last and went to their separate beds, each with a new-found subject for dreams.

Tony hoped and Amy feared that a new phase of their relationship would be opening, but when they met again at breakfast the habits of years were re-established and they slipped back into Platonic friendship, on Amy's part at least.

Apart from the one, unregretted extravagance of the marquee dance, Tony's allowance had almost no calls on it and had been supplemented by an unexpected gift of conscience money from his mother. Finding himself unexpectedly still in funds, he seized the opportunity offered by a break in the dinner-time chatter to ask Mr Fergusson if he could arrange for a few gliding lessons from a qualified instructor. "I'm not too young to make a start, am I?"

"Certainly not." Mr Fergusson put down his fork. "I think it could be arranged," he said. As he spoke, he saw the sudden yearning in his daughter's eyes and remembered an approach that had been made that morning on behalf of the proprietor of a chain of newspapers, enquiring whether he would be interested in providing long- and short-term local forecasts for all his papers. It was pie in the sky for the moment but it would be money in the bank if it came off, in which case he would have to break a long-standing habit of thinking himself almost on the breadline. It was certainly worth a gamble – a place in his daughter's good books against the possibility of having to give up his own gliding for a period if the deal fell through. "Perhaps it's time for your instruction to begin," he told Amy. "Just two or three lessons to begin with," he added quickly.

Amy, who had waited so long that hope had begun to fade, was dumb-struck, but she jumped to her feet and kissed her father on his bald spot. That event, now that she was becoming a young lady, was such a rarity that he too was afraid to mark the occasion with gracious words. Instead, he said, "I'll see if Derek Cardinal can take you both on. He's very good and he enjoys instructing the young."

"The novelist?" they said in unison.

"Why not? He's a qualified instructor. A bit eccentric at times, perhaps. If he starts talking to himself, he's just writing dialogue in his head. He's been doing more gliding and instructing than writing these last few years since his wife died. I have lunch with him at the club now and again, just two old widowers together, putting the world to rights."

Amy looked at Tony. His eyes were popping. "But that would be . . ." she began. She hesitated. It was not an occasion for annoying her father with any of the contemporary slang words of approval which were stolen from other contexts and thus made unusable by post-adolescents. "Wonderful," she finished.

Two days later, Mr Fergusson confirmed that an appointment had been made and on the due day he drove them to the airstrip and introduced them to a small, frail-looking man with thinning grey hair and a deeply grooved face. Derek Cardinal looked much older than the distinguished-looking man in the photograph on the dust-jacket of *Unsafe Haven*, but, Amy reminded herself, the book had been written years earlier and followed since by four or five more. The intervening years had not flattered him but had given him a puckish, mischievous look. He shook hands politely with each of his new pupils.

Amy's father had no intention of being left out in the cold when extravagance was the order of the day. He excused himself and went to enter himself on the Flying List in order to book an aerotow launch.

Mr Cardinal might be well blessed with years but he was still cheerful and full of energy. He led them briskly out to the launch point, where the glider was waiting. This time, Amy noticed, it was the other two-seater with seats in tandem. It was the two-seater with the better aerodynamics, but it meant that Mr Cardinal would be

addressing his instructions to the back of her neck. Her
father had made much use of hand gestures in conveying
his meaning.

"We'll run through the pre-flight briefing together,"
Cardinal said. "Then you can toss a coin to decide
which of you comes up first." He raised the canopy
and reached into the cockpit for the Daily Inspection
Book. "I'm checking to see that the glider has undergone
its Daily Inspection," he explained. "Then I look at the
Certificate of Airworthiness Placard and the Limitations
Placard, making sure that the C of A hasn't expired. You
do this every time you take over a glider. OK so far?"

"Yes," said Amy. Tony said, "No problem."

"Next," said Mr Cardinal, "a little instruction in the use
of the one item which has something in common with the
cowboy's gun. You hope you'll never need it, but if you
need it you'll need it in a hurry and you'd better do it
right. The parachute."

"We know about that," Tony said. "Mr Fergusson
taught us."

Mr Cardinal's cheery manner suffered a slight eclipse.
"Mr Fergusson," he said gently, "is a fine man and a good
flier, so I'm sure that you do know all about it. However,
while I'm your instructor I prefer to teach you my way.
There's only one tow-plane today and we have a little
time in hand before we come to the top of the Flying List.
It's better that I teach it to you seventeen times when you
already know how to use the parachute than that you ever
have to use it and suddenly find that you've forgotten.
If we have to jump, I shall say 'Evacuate, evacuate!'
He smiled suddenly, bringing a gleam of youth to his

63

well-worn, elfin face. "In point of fact I shall say it three times, but you'll only hear it twice because by the time I get around to the third I shall be out of there and on the way down. So I won't be around to help you out."

Tony laughed and said that he was sorry. They were instructed afresh in the use of the parachute and remained silent while Mr Cardinal explained the controls. Amy, remembering that a glider cockpit can function much like a greenhouse, was wearing light clothing and she felt the breeze cool on her back.

"While we wait," Mr Cardinal said, "I'll ask you a riddle. Which costs more to buy, the tow-plane or the glider?"

"The tow-plane, surely," Tony said after a pause.

"And why?"

"Well, because it has an engine and things."

"Some time soon," said Mr Cardinal, "we'll take a good look at a tow-plane and compare it with a competition glider. You'll see that the glider has to be much lighter because it needs a very shallow gliding angle. It's altogether very much more high-tech, more lightly constructed, better finished and consequently both more expensive and more delicate than the plane. So that's the first instalment of Lesson One. A glider is handled with all the care you would give to a very old lady who you were still expecting to change her Will in your favour."

Tony won the toss and decided to fly first. Amy was told to stay where she was so she sat down and leaned back against a small stack of tyres, in the sun but sheltered from the breeze, while the tow-plane arrived along with a 'wing-holder' – a man on foot whose duty it was to balance the glider by supporting one wing until the glider was moving and under control. The cable was attached to the glider. The sound of the plane's engine increased and they moved away and rose without apparent effort into the air. Soon, the glider seemed to have vanished, but Amy was content to enjoy the day and watch the ever-changing scene.

She was admiring the smooth touchdown of one of the privately-owned gliders when a shadow fell across her. She looked up, twisting her head and squinting against the sun, to recognise Mrs Hogweed, the wife of one of the most enthusiastic members of the club. Mrs Hogweed was somewhere in her thirties (although to Amy she seemed almost as old as Derek Cardinal). She was gifted with a baby-doll face, blonde hair and a figure which was little short of voluptuous.

"Are you waiting for Mr Cardinal?" she asked.

Amy was surprised by the antipathy in the woman's voice but she replied politely that she was.

"Which glider are you getting?"

"The tandem."

"That's good. Much less temptation for wandering hands."

Without another word, Mrs Hogweed strode off towards the hanger, leaving Amy perplexed. Surely that nice, respectable, *old* man was not in the habit of groping women? She gave a mental shrug. Time enough to worry about that if it happened. His books had given her so much enjoyment that she was prepared to make allowances.

The tow-plane returned and gave the other waiting gliders their launch, but it was half an hour before the elongated two-seat glider touched down gently at the downwind end of the runway, rolled and then gently dipped a wing as it came to a halt. The two figures climbed out. A small group of members helped to push the glider, tail-first, back to the launch point.

"I'll see you back in the clubhouse," Mr Cardinal said to Tony, smiling, as Amy arrived. The tow-plane was taxiing towards them. "It seems to be our turn again." He helped her to adjust the parachute, but without once going beyond what Amy considered to be the bounds of propriety. "Hop in, young lady. You should be able to adjust the rudder pedals to suit your dimensions. It's not too cramped."

Amy, suddenly nervous, was conscious that she was in the presence of a successful writer. She was also unsettled by Mrs Hogweed's remark. She had been studying *Romeo and Juliet* at school. "''Tis not so deep as a well,'" she said, "'nor so wide as a church-door; but 'tis enough, 'twill serve.'" And for no good reason, she added the words which were destined to have a disproportionate effect on her life. "As Shakespeare said."

Derek Cardinal looked at her sharply. "If that's what you want to believe," he said, "I can't stop you. In you get and if we can't 'put a girdle round about the earth in forty minutes', we can at least go part-way."

Amy settled into the front seat. A minute later, the launch-point controller gave the signal and they were rolling. As they lifted off, the rumble of the main wheel became the silence of flight and Amy felt the familiar stirring of joy. At 2,000 feet, Mr Cardinal released the tow-rope and the plane banked away. "You have control," his voice came from behind her.

Experience with her father stood Amy in good stead. She took a gentle grip of the control column and found that the glider was trimmed to settle in a shallow glide. On her instructor's command, she circled left and then right. Evidently her performance was satisfactory. Through the column she could feel his grip on the dual control relax. "Your father tells me that you're shaping up as a meteorologist," he said. "Where would you go, to prolong the flight?"

Amy had been looking around. "There are two gliders circling under that cloud," she said. "I think they've found a thermal."

"Go and join them. And remember to keep an all-round lookout at all times. Your only risk now is of colliding with another aircraft, which can only happen if you don't keep using your eyes."

Spiralling upward in a thermal was a more delicate balancing act than executing simple turns, but Mr Cardinal was a good instructor. His advice was calm and lucid. Amy could feel her own tension spilling out of her. Soon, on top of the thrill of having such a machine responding to her commands, she became able even to admire the beauty of the day, the glow of sunshine on the hills and the crawling shadows of the clouds. When the thermal died, he told her to fly back towards the airstrip. He resumed control while they were still a mile out and he brought the glider in, to a landing as gentle as a lover's kiss.

They disembarked, helped push the glider back to the launch point and handed over the glider to another instructor. "Now," Mr Cardinal said, "we'll have a coffee and I'll take you both through what you should have learned but perhaps didn't take in."

As they walked back towards the distant clubhouse, Amy wanted to say how much she enjoyed his books, but her nerve failed her. Instead, she asked him, "What did you mean about Shakespeare?"

He thought for a moment, slowing his pace. "I meant that you can believe whatever you want to believe. We'll never find proof positive now – classical plays went out of favour during the Restoration and many of his personal details were lost for ever."

"Proof?" Amy said. "I don't understand. Proof of what?"

"Proof as to who wrote the plays." He slowed his pace. "Let's pause for a minute." They settled on a teak seat presented to the club by the widow of a former member. Amy sat well out of reach but Mr Cardinal seemed not to notice.

"William Shakespeare," he said, "was educated at the local school. It was a good enough school. He could have become a schoolmaster. But, although there are about six years unaccounted for, there's no record that he ever had any further education. Most probably he was apprenticed to his father, the glove-maker. At about twenty-one, following the probably apocryphal poaching incident, he ran off to London and his first job at the theatre seems to have been holding horses outside it. Yet within comparatively few years he became an actor and raised the money to partner the Burbages in building the Globe Theatre. He must have been a busy lad. Yet the plays show a remarkable knowledge of the law, medicine, geography, history, mythology, you name it. Even allowing that he pinched some of his plots from early Italian sources, how did he find the time for research, let alone write an average of two major plays a year for twenty years?

"Bear in mind also that there's no record of him calling himself a playwright and no reference to his plays in the famous will. Nor have any fragments of the plays turned up in a handwriting resembling the rather illiterate hand that wrote the four signatures on that will.

"One final point. When you get home, I suggest that you take some politician's speech, or the editorial in your newspaper, and try to turn it into iambic pentameters, sticking to the simple one-two rhythm of the blank verse and not allowing yourself the occasional dactyl as did the Latin poets." Glancing sideways he saw that Amy was looking bemused. "Dactyl?" he said. "Dumdiddy. Waltz rhythm. Try it and see how long it takes you. Note that the exercise defeated even that genius. One of the greatest pieces of oratory in the English language begins with a series of dactyls. 'Friends, Romans, countrymen, lend me your ears.' But when you've tried for yourself, then tell me whether you still believe that a busy actor-manager and businessman could find the time to write two such plays a year. And now, young Tony will be wondering where we've got to."

As they neared the clubhouse Amy found the courage to tell him how much she admired his books. He showed embarrassment and for once his rolling periods died away.

"When I'm God," Amy said sleepily, "I'm going to do

away with all this Christmas nonsense and let people give each other presents whenever they feel like it."

"God now, is it?" Tony retorted. "Is there no limit to this girl's ambition?"

"That particular ambition would seem to be self-limiting," Mr Fergusson remarked. "Within the bounds of our present understanding, it would seem that there'd be nowhere to go but down."

"Exactly," said Tony, as though that had been his point all along. "Imagine having to be right every time. And not being able to speak to anybody without them wetting themselves and dashing out to quote every word and be canonised. Anyway, there's never been a female God yet."

"Of course there has," said Amy. "Have. Starting away back. The Egyptians had loads of them. So did the Greeks and Romans. We wouldn't have the word goddess if there weren't any."

Julia Mason was acquiring the wavelength of their zany arguments. Start with an impossible proposition and then follow it through to the logical conclusion. "Anyway, I don't see that a god of one religion could do away with something from another," she said. "I mean, it would hardly do for Buddha to lift the Catholic embargo on eating meat on Fridays."

"It happens all the time," Amy said repressively.

The four were stretched out in easy chairs in front of a log fire. The comfortable sitting room of Firhaven was lit only by the dance of the flames and a flicker from the television which was silently presenting the image of some faraway and long-past game show.

Julia was a friend, though not a very close friend, of Amy's from school. Her parents, a pair of wildlife film-makers, were to be away in some equatorial graveyard through December and it had been planned that Julia would spend the school holiday with an aunt whom she detested. Her grumbles against this fate had been so petulant that in the end Amy had pressed her father to issue an invitation, which had been quickly accepted.

Mr Fergusson was enjoying the company and the availability of three teenagers to take over the bulk of the chores. Amy, for her part, was beginning to regret her compassionate impulse. Not only did she have to share her bedroom (Mr Fergusson having taken over the fourth bedroom as an annexe to his study) but Julia's presence was a constant intrusion between herself and Tony – indeed, as soon as she realised that Tony was heir to the estate next door, Julia's manner had become openly flirtatious. The phrase 'Tony and I' had become firmly established in her conversation. Tony, moreover, had shown no distaste for being waited on by two attractive girls only a year younger than himself. Julia was a compact and slightly chubby girl with piquant features, glowing red hair, freckles and good legs which were often on generous display. Perhaps it was a coincidence, but Tony was showing signs of the self-confidence which he had previously lacked and Amy was annoyed that the gift should come from Julia.

As the two girls were preparing for bed that night – an event which would have driven Tony to the verge of madness if he had happened to witness it – Julia suddenly asked, "Have you done all your Christmas shopping?"

Amy's Christmas shopping was finished, wrapped, labelled and hidden at the bottom of her underwear drawer, but the question aroused her suspicions. "Most of it," she said cautiously. "Why?"

"Nothing much. Tony and I" – Amy's teeth snapped together – "thought we might go to the Springburn Shopping Centre tomorrow."

"It's an awful journey," Amy said. "The bus tours around every little hamlet along the way and Dad's car goes in for servicing tomorrow, so he couldn't take us even if he wanted to, which he wouldn't."

"Tony said that he'd get his father's chauffeur to run us in or else he'd spring for a taxi."

Tony was as good as his word. Amy suddenly remembered some urgent shopping in need of her attention. Several of Mr Hope-Williams's small fleet of cars were stored in the Hall garages but the only qualified chauffeur was Mr Andrews Junior who was laid up with the flu. The three went by taxi to a larger town some ten miles away, where not only was the shopping better but the best shops were clustered under one roof. Amy, sensing that her own modest present for Tony had better be supplemented by something a little more lavish if she were not to be outshone, had begged some extra money from her father. In the town's premier bookshop, she bought the most elaborate, the most expensive and up-to-date book on gliding that she could find.

By that time, Julia and Tony had disappeared. She found them at last. Tony was looking a bit frayed at having his opinion sought over every least frippery that Julia considered purchasing and he was easily persuaded to ally himself with Amy in calling a halt to the expedition. During the journey back, Julia chattered happily, but the others were silent, looking out on a seasonable but unwelcome fall of snow. Tony and Amy, but for different reasons, each felt that Julia had outstayed her welcome.

Next morning, a cold but bright sun shone across a sparkling landscape. Trees were bowed with the weight of snow. The sky looked navy blue against such whiteness. Amy stole a quick word with Tony. Then she addressed Julia across the breakfast table. "Tony and I," she said with relish, "thought that we'd get in a little driving practice. You can join us if you like."

The Suzuki, lovingly repainted by hand in a colour more suitable for a fire appliance, awaited them in one of the outbuildings at the Hall. The engine started without trouble. For want of driving licences, car tax and insurance, it was first necessary to walk from the gates of the Hall driveway to the service station and return, each carrying a gallon can of petrol. Tony and Amy, being well provided with clothes suitable for the country in winter, relished the brisk walk and threw snowballs. Their breath smoked in the frosty air. Julia was fretful.

Most of the drives and estate roads were bordered on one side or the other by a hedge or fence, so there was no great difficulty in following them despite the snow. Julia had had informal driving lessons from her father. At first, they were content to take it in turns to drive, groping their way around in four-wheel drive, but this soon palled. The snow packed down and as the routes became clearly marked by wheel-tracks they also became icy. Tony began to twist the car through the bends in a series of slow-motion skids, on a neutral throttle and with much correction by the steering-wheel. Amy then selected two-wheel drive and took it a stage further by discovering for herself the classic power-slide, steering the car by careful adjustments of the throttle. Immediately, nothing would satisfy Tony but to take over the wheel again and after one wild excursion – luckily onto level grass – he mastered the new technique.

Julia, cramped into the back, protested sulkily that the others were hogging all the fun. There was some truth in the assertion. Rather guiltily, they rearranged themselves with Amy in the back. Amy explained the basic physics involved. Tony gave practical directions. Immediately, the relationship of Tony-and-I became re-established, replacing the joyous laughter which had prevailed. Amy was a silent back-seat passenger while Tony, his patience beginning to wear thin, drove by proxy. Julia began to grasp the technique but progressed little further than to approach each bend slowly, apply a little steering and then kick the tail round with little cries of self-congratulation and pleas for Tony's approval.

At school, Amy had admired Julia for her air of sophistication and her slightly raunchy but probably apocryphal stories, but here in her own environment she could see the other for a dangerous and disloyal harpy. Moreover, she was bored. Making sure that the movement caught Julia's eye in the driving mirror, Amy yawned hugely and then closed her eyes as if for sleep.

It was enough and more than enough. The result far exceeded Amy's intention. Julia clamped her jaw tightly and tackled the next bend too fast. Then, suddenly afraid to hit the throttle, she trod on the brakes. The world outside did wonderful gyrations as the car spun and left the drive. Fortunately there were no trees nearby but there was a grassy slope down to a level field. The car descended at an angle. It almost remained upright but its narrow wheel-base was against it. It reached the bottom of the bank, where the snow lay in a knee-high drift, and rolled over gently onto its roof. Both doors flew open. Tony climbed hastily over Julia to reach the ignition.

Tony and Julia had only to let themselves fall out. Amy, inverted, was suddenly unable to remember how to unlock the seat-backs but she managed to wriggle between the head-rests and what had once been the roof. As Amy emerged, Tony said urgently, "Petrol will be leaking out. I can smell it. And oil."

"And battery acid," said Amy. "Quick, roll her back onto her wheels."

They forced the doors more or less closed. Under the snow there was still a slope in their favour. Between them, Tony and Amy could almost right the car, but the weight and the snow underfoot defeated them and it fell back. "Come on," Tony snapped at Julia. "Help us."

"I've hurt my hand," Julia said.

Tony's patience popped. "You've hurt my car more. Come on, you stupid cow, use the other hand. *Heave!*"

Julia began a lengthy protest but she added her strength to the effort. The car began to surrender. It turned onto its side and, with a great creaking of snow, rolled half-way towards righting itself. But Julia's feet slipped and she fell full length in the snow. The car began to roll back, pressing her down into the drift but, with an enormous effort, Tony and Amy managed to complete the roll and return the Suzuki to its wheels.

In the deep imprint left by the car, something stirred. Julia extracted herself, one limb at a time, and got to her feet, one-handedly dislodging snow from all over her person and spitting slush.

"Look." Tony said. "An abominable snowman."

"You're not supposed to say that," Amy told him. "It's not PC. You should say 'an abominable snow-person'." Julia raised her voice stridently, breathing steam. She had *never* been spoken to like that before and she thought her wrist was broken and nobody cared and she wasn't going to spend another day in a house where people treated people like that, she would rather go to her aunt who was a holy terror but a darling compared to *some* people who thought they were very funny. She set off towards Firhaven, floundering through the snow, but her voice died away only slowly in the frozen air.

Tony ignored it. "If Suzie's still running," he said, "we'd better try to get her back under cover where we can bash out the worst of the damage." He picked up a window-glass which had fallen out and dropped it on the back seat. "Poor Suzie," he said. "Do you think she was trying to tell us something?"

"Suzie? Yes, I think she probably was," Amy said.

They set to work again, in perfect harmony. Two against the world.

Shortly before her eighteenth birthday, Amy gained her 'A' Badge from the British Gliding Association by flying, white-knuckled and solo in her father's glider, once

around the airstrip, making a perfect landing and answering some questions about the Rules of the Air. Three
months later, she obtained her 'B' Badge by maintaining a soaring flight. For this, five minutes would have
sufficed but Amy found a thermal too strong to spurn
and stayed aloft for nearly two hours, following the
thermal up through the sunshine above the clouds and
then descending as slowly as she could manage, all to
her delight and Mr Cardinal's great consternation.

He was waiting for her when she landed. He had already
placed himself in the area where a descending glider was
likely to come to a halt and he arrived at a brisk jog-trot
as she opened the canopy. "Where have you been?" he
demanded. (Amy decided that it was a silly question in the
circumstances – there was only one place where she could
have been. But she could see that he was upset.) "We've
been phoning all over the place for you. We thought that
you must have run out of lift and come down in a field
somewhere."

Amy's euphoria faded and she felt immediately guilty.
"Well, I'm sorry. But I was paying for the tow and you
didn't say that it had to be a quickie. And then, when
I set course for home, the damnedest thing happened. I
seemed to hear a crowd of people behind me, jabbering
away, but I couldn't make out a word. I looked round to
see if Tony had left a transistor radio in the cockpit. But it
was a skein of large geese, Greenland whitefronts I think.
They'd formed up on me as their leader and they stayed in
formation until I began to descend over the airstrip. Does
that happen often?"

"I only heard of it once before."

"I take it as a compliment, then. Anyway, you're the one who showed me how to make the most of a narrow thermal by banking hard and circling tight, to gain lift from the air being drawn in, so it's all your fault for teaching me so well. Does it count as one of the soaring flights for my bronze badge?"

Only slightly mollified, Mr Cardinal said that he supposed so. He helped return the glider to the hangar and then made for the clubhouse at a pace whose briskness betrayed his continuing chagrin. Amy hurried to catch up and, when common courtesy forced him to slow down, fell into step with him. She sought for a different subject, to jolly him back into his usual kind and courteous self. "About Shakespeare," she said suddenly. "Who do *you* think wrote the plays? Francis Bacon?"

Mr Cardinal uttered a sound that put Amy in mind of a hen laying a square egg, but he shifted instantly from gloom to academic disdain. "That was mostly in the fevered imagination of Delia Bacon, an American poetess and no relation to Francis, Viscount St Albans, although she was no doubt intrigued by the coincidence of names. Bacon was a busy Lord Chancellor with a quite different style of writing. He was an essayist rather than a poet. And he would have had no reason to hide his light under a bushel. No, if you're seeking the real author you must look for somebody with a first class education, a talent for blank verse, time on his hands and a good reason to have somebody else put his name to the plays."

They were nearing the clubhouse. "Who, then?" Amy asked desperately.

"Try Christopher Marlowe. He was a contemporary,

78

born the same year as Shakespeare. But most authorities refer to him as a forerunner of Shakespeare, or some such words. Read his *Tamburlaine*. Or, better, *The Jew of Malta*. With a little ingenuity, you'll find that you can interpose bits of Marlowe and bits of Shakespeare and be unable to remember which is which. And," he added, "don't you ever give me a fright like that again. Tell your father to get a radio for his glider."

Amy, still smarting from the rebuke, headed for home while Mr Cardinal, in the clubhouse, made an amusing story out of Amy's prolonged flight and the excuses that she had given him.

Tony obtained his 'B' badge only a few weeks later, but he was obviously miffed that Amy had preceded him to that award. And so Amy waited until he had obtained his driving licence before sitting the test herself. She could not gloss over the fact, however, that she had passed at the first attempt while he had needed two bites at the cherry.

Tony was already enrolled in the London School of Economics but was still spending with the Fergussons as many of his vacations as he could manage without seriously damaging his relationships with his parents. His mother, however, was in the throes of a second divorce and, suddenly recalling her firstborn, was demanding of his support and comfort.

Amy, meantime, was leaving school with a university place already certain. Julia had been spreading scurrilous stories about her stay as a guest of the Fergussons. During the last few days of the school term, Amy took her revenge by hiding all Julia's underwear on the morning of a breezy summer's day and, because Julia had not made herself loved, had no difficulty in persuading all their contemporaries to refuse to lend any replacements. The consequences were considered insupportable by the victim and hilarious by the rest of the school. The two erstwhile friends parted without regret on either side.

Once she was enrolled at university, Amy's life changed radically. Her studies she found to be well within her capabilities, but life in student digs was itself a culture shock after boarding school. There would have been little opportunity for gliding even if her father, still bearing most of the cost of her education, had been able to afford it.

Instead, she joined the local sailing club, expecting no more than to crew for others in occasional dinghy races. But talent has a way of advertising itself. It was not long before word went around that there was a club member whose predictions of wind speed and direction were more detailed, more local and often more accurate than those otherwise obtainable. Amy was in immediate demand.

She wrote to Tony:

. . . any fool can tell what the weather's probably going to do, it's forecasting *when* that gets difficult. I have Dad's latest program, extrapolating from every known past pattern, in my laptop plus floppies. It's red hot, and I only have to phone him for Met Office data in the morning. Result: invited to crew regularly on big racing yacht belonging Sir Charles Aylmer and Lady Aylmer. Explained studies have to come first in term-time (and still need earn pin-money in vacations) but go when I can. Expected to do watches with the rest, but don't have the strength of these rugger-buggers so let off lightly and do cooking instead. Different knack in small galley and bouncing boat but getting hang of it. *Cordon bleu* very much appreciated provided it comes between two halves of bun for eating on watch.

Already pulled weight, one time I wasn't even aboard, by forecasting offshore gale. Sent telegram. *Laughing Girl* hugged coast while others blown miles offshore, won hands down. Sir Charles sent me case champagne, sweet old-fashioned thing. Sailing's same kind of fun as gliding but takes pretty much for ever and costs the earth.

Who was Saint Tropez anyway?

Tony wrote from St Tropez:

You'd love it here, the yachts are fantastic. Dad came over, weekend, thought of buying big one 'til he heard what they cost. Turned white and hand shook. Insists I go study at Harvard Business School, when finish at LSE. Not keen, especially as he's talking about arrangements for me to spend vacs over there. Wouldn't have got where he is if he hadn't known the value of a pound (and dollar and Deutschmark and all the other currencies) but promising generous allowance and amazing goodies if I go all the way. Want try for FAI Silver Badge, but time will run out on me.

Saint Tropez? No idea. Probably turned wine back into water. The French are good at that.

*   *   *

Amy found some adequately paid vacation work with the local leisure centre. Despite her sailing activities and study commitments, by living at a frenetic pace she still managed to cram some gliding into her crowded schedule.

Her father brought her to the Christmas dinner-dance of the Gliding Club. By arrangement, they shared their table with Derek Cardinal and a male pupil of Mr Cardinal's who, Amy gathered, had been brought along for her benefit. To Amy's relief, however, the young man, who quite failed to attract her, proved much more interested in the daughter of the Club Secretary – a bleached blonde in a dress so diaphanous that the absence of any brassière beneath it was evident on less than careful scrutiny. There was some muttering among the wives of the senior members.

Late in the evening, while her unfaithful date was in a clinch on the dance-floor with the blonde, but barely moving more than enough to generate a little pleasurable friction between them, and Mr Fergusson was doing his duty by the President's wife, Mr Cardinal enquired without enthusiasm whether Amy would care to dance. Amy was popular with the younger members and had already danced until her new slippers with their unaccustomed heels were pinching her insteps. She had also noticed that Mr Cardinal was not a very good dancer although, watching closely, she could see no sign of the wandering hands against which Mrs Hogweed had warned her. "I'd just as soon sit and chat," she said.

Mr Cardinal glowered at his other pupil, who had now arrived as close to fornication with the blonde as was possible on the dance-floor without inviting arrest. "I also," he said. "I've long ceased trying to convince myself that I enjoy moving around to the sound of music. Even the pleasure of getting to grips with lovelies such as yourself hardly makes up for the tenderness in the joints next day, the consequence of the passing years."

Amy began to wonder whether there mightn't be something in Mrs Hogweed's suspicions after all. She decided to steer the conversation back to safer ground. "I enjoyed your last book," she said. "Latest, I mean."

"Thank you. But you were nearly right," he said. He took a large sip from his brandy. It was not his first drink. "Last book but one, I think. I have one more left in me. After that, I retire."

Amy searched for and found yet another topic. "I read up on Christopher Marlowe," she said. "But I don't see how he could have written the Shakespearean plays. He was murdered in a tavern brawl when the plays had hardly started being produced."

He blinked at her in the owlish manner of the slightly fuddled. "You're sure of that?"

"It's what the books say."

"Oh, books! You don't want to believe everything you read in books." He leaned forward and put his elbows on the table, nearly spilling his drink. "Marlowe was a brilliant youth, very well educated, Cambridge MA, but wild. More than wild – wicked. Among other things, if he was here now I might introduce him to you but probably not to that nephew of mine."

"He was gay?"

"It's not certain but it seems probable. He and Shakespeare

certainly met. During their brief overlap they seem both to have been working for Lord Strange's actors.

"Let me set the scene for you." Derek Cardinal lit a small cigar and waved away the smoke. The light of the fanatic was in his eyes. "At the tail end of the sixteenth century, two major schisms were tearing the country apart. Mary Tudor had tried to return the country to Catholicism. Now Elizabeth was determined to stamp Catholicism out once and for all. Just why anybody should give a damn how if at all somebody else worships is quite beyond me," he added reflectively, "but at the time it was very literally a life and death issue. Catholic plots for invasion or assassination – real, imaginary or deliberately provoked – were legion. The Babington Plot, which cost Mary Queen of Scots her life, was set in motion for that purpose by Walsingham, Elizabeth's spymaster, who was adept at that sort of entrapment.

"This was the infancy of modern espionage. Spies abounded on both sides, and because the consequence of being caught was likely to be torture and execution, they were easily turned. But there was no certain way to be sure which side such a man was really on. Some were undoubtedly on both sides at once. Their motive was money.

"At the same time, the Earl of Essex and Sir Walter Raleigh were at daggers drawn over who was to be the queen's favourite with all the power and privilege entailed. Raleigh had the advantage until his marriage to one of Elizabeth's ladies-in-waiting became known. Then he fell from favour. In the end, each of them was executed but, at the time we're concerned with, Essex was determined to complete his rival's downfall. Raleigh was still too big a target to attack directly, but he could be got at through his friend and protégé, Christopher Marlowe."

Cardinal broke off and signalled to a waiter.

"I wish I'd had you for a teacher when I was doing History," Amy said sincerely. "My teachers made history sound boring but, when you tell it, these are real people. Do go on."

When a waiter had taken the order, Cardinal resumed. "Marlowe was a known and outspoken atheist. It was claimed that he had 'read the atheist lecture to Sir Walter Raleigh and others'. There was a determined effort by Essex's agents to frame Marlowe on a host of charges, to get him imprisoned and tortured, expecting that he would bring Raleigh down with him. But the plot failed, largely due to the intervention of another of Marlowe's protectors, Sir Robert Cecil. Marlowe was arrested but he was freed on bail, which suggests that the charges weren't taken too seriously. One theory is that Marlowe was killed because he was now a danger."

"But you, of course, have a better theory?" Amy suggested.

"Judge for yourself. Marlowe was getting heavily into debt. As I said, he knew Shakespeare. I can just imagine a conversation. 'Listen, Bill,' says Marlowe, 'my classical plays are doing good business but I don't get to keep any of the dosh, my creditors snaffle it first. How would you like to produce *Titus Andronicus* under your own name and split the take?' Shakespeare was already thinking about raising money towards the Globe Theatre, so he's keen. 'Cool,' he says."

Amy giggled at the imagery but her imagination was caught. "That still doesn't explain the fact that most of the plays were written after he was dead."

"But was he really dead? After the first couple of plays were produced, Marlowe was in trouble. Potentially, he *was* trouble. He had been arrested. His atheistic blasphemies were a matter of record. And very conveniently he goes to Deptford with three doubtful characters out of his past, men who would do anything for money. But it wasn't to a tavern, it was the house of a widow, a Mrs Eleanor Bull. He ends up knifed, according to their story, after an argument.

"Remember, there was no forensic science in those days and no CID. There was an inquest in front of the coroner. The friends said that the body was that of Christopher Marlowe and they told their story. Why would he disbelieve them? But it was a plague year – bodies would be easy to come by. The jury brought in a verdict of murder against one of the men but he was never prosecuted. Instead, there's a record of a royal pardon for the killer, Frizer, on grounds of self-defence. That, in particular, seems unlikely. Marlowe had a reputation for being aggressive, but his aggression seems to have been verbal, not physical.

"Marlowe had some powerful friends. Raleigh, Cecil, the Walsinghams. Devious men. Plotters and schemers. But the one who interests me is Henry Percy, Earl of Northumberland. A studious man with a vast library and one of the very few who later lived to a ripe old age.

"As I said before, you can believe what you want to believe. But which do you think more likely – the less educated Shakespeare somehow finding time to research and write an average of two major plays a year for twenty years while acting and conducting business, travelling to and from Stratford and fathering at least one child along the way; or the much better educated Marlowe, whisked away by his powerful friends, who provided a suitable corpse and stage-managed the whole business, to spend the rest of his days in retirement on the Earl of Northumberland's estate, with free access to a large library, writing like mad?"

"I see what you mean," Amy said doubtfully.

It seemed to Amy that Mr Cardinal was watching her closely. "But you don't believe? Or you believe but don't approve?"

"I think it was a bit tough on the creditors," Amy said. "Otherwise . . . I suppose it was one answer to a problem."

Mr Cardinal nodded slowly. "We'll discuss it again," he said. Amy thought that he was looking at her speculatively and she moved further out of reach.

Five

Tony managed to arrange one more summer vacation with the Fergussons between graduating at the London School of Economics and being bundled off to Harvard. His father had rewarded a satisfactory conclusion at the LSE with unusual generosity and Mr Fergusson's client list had expanded satisfactorily, so the two could afford to spend at least a portion of the time aloft. Each was aiming for the bronze badge of the British Gliding Association. The soaring and check flights presented little difficulty and Amy soon had the coveted badge, but Tony, who had had, for the moment, what he called a 'bellyful of book-work', boggled at the necessary study of Air Law, Navigation and Meteorology, and only with considerable coaching from Amy managed to complete the written test paper shortly before his departure to the States was due.

They were lolling in the deck chairs one evening. Rooks high overhead were heading to roost. The garden was tidy and smelled ravishing. "It says in the paper," Amy began drowsily, "that in the year something-or-other we'll all be standing shoulder to shoulder like sardines and yet we put a whole lot of medical resources into fertility pills and IVF. When I'm President of the World—"

"I've heard of ambition, but this is *folie de grandeur*," Tony said. "Anyway, the world doesn't have a president."

"It'll come," Amy said. "Bound to. We can't have you economists rocking the boat much longer."

"Hey! We're the ones who keep the boat steady, remember?"

Amy roused herself. "Rubbish! Think about it. Money stops the right things being done because you economists prophesy doom and disaster to national economies if anyone ever did anything sensible. Do you think it's reasonable that some governments pay farmers to produce less while much of the world is starving? That billions of man-hours are needed to make the world a better place, yet hordes of graduates can't get jobs? And we still haven't found a way to stop dictatorships slaughtering their own people. World government's got to come."

"If it ever happens the politicians will make a total hash of it. I'm going to bed. Good night, Mr Fergusson." Ignoring Amy, Tony stumped into the house.

Mr Fergusson had been listening to the exchange with a faint smile. Now he said, "You want to go easy on that young man."

"I'm very fond of Tony, but he does get on my . . ." Amy paused, unsure whether she should say 'tits' in front of her father. It sometimes seemed to her that he had led a sheltered life. "Up my nose sometimes," she substituted. "He gets so cocky."

"He's driven to boast occasionally," her father agreed. "But that's only because he feels insecure."

"I don't see what he's got to feel insecure about. A rich father, a degree from the LSE and work waiting for him."

"Think about it," her father suggested. "He's grown up in the shadow of a domineering father who expects too much of him. He's caught in a vicious circle. He has few friends so, feeling left out, he falls into a common trap and takes to boasting – which loses him the friends he might have made. I've been watching the pair of you. You're his only real friend. He values your friendship, but you seem to trump his aces. He takes you fishing, but you catch the fish. His academic results are good, but you equal them and you're a year younger than he is. And whenever he puts on a bit of side – trying to convince himself, not you – you slap him down."

"I don't really, do I?" Amy asked.

"I'm afraid you do. Try to build him up rather than knock him down. Otherwise you'll lose him. His friendship, I mean. Whatever you do, don't over-react and be nicer to him than you think your old father would wish. Enough said. I'm going to bed and I suggest that you do the same – alone."

On the last evening of his visit, Tony and Amy walked to a favourite pub a mile from Firhaven. Mr Fergusson was invited to accompany them but he guessed that the invitation had been no more than a courtesy and he declined, hiding a gleam of amusement.

The two lingered rather longer than they had intended

and daylight was almost gone before they set off for home. The road lights were competing with a seemingly enormous moon above the rooftops. Their way led between cottage gardens so that the scent of flowers was all around. The whole scene was almost cloyingly romantic and this may have encouraged Tony to be more outgoing than his usual.

His arm was around her waist and he tightened his clasp. "It's been another brilliant interlude," he said. "I'm heart-broken that it's over. Almost."

Amy wanted to ask whether he meant that he was almost heart-broken or that the interlude was almost over, but she could guess the direction in which he was trying to drag the conversation and, on balance, preferred to postpone it. "We haven't done much together," she said. "Half the time, one of us has been on the ground and looking up, wondering where the other's got to. No more bicycle races. Not much fishing."

"It's been too hot and bright for trout to rise," Tony said. "And poor old Suzie had to go to the scrapyard. But we've had no mishaps. Neither of us has injured the other, which is a step forward, and . . . and I think we've had a lot of fun."

"You'll be back," Amy said.

"Not for ages. Dad expects me to spend the short vacs over there, studying or making useful contacts. You'll go on writing to me and sending photographs?" he asked anxiously.

Amy was surprised that he asked. "Yes, of course," she said.

The front garden of Firhaven was partly screened by a

large clump of mature rhododendrons. Tony drew Amy into the privacy of the shadows. Amy did not resist. Her original determination to limit physical contact between them to an occasional peck on the lips had gradually weakened, as such resolutions are wont to do. The two had exchanged caresses, in a friendly rather than an amorous way, and Amy had been forced to do what at first she had avoided – drawing a line which had to be re-drawn at intervals. But, though she was aware of Tony's excitement and occasionally felt what she thought must be rising passion in herself, she had stoutly refused to progress beyond the point at which a moderately liberated mother might have raised her voice in protest. If she was being seduced, she thought suddenly, the seduction was slow enough to figure in the *Guinness Book of Records*. She shook momentarily with secret laughter.

"What's so funny?" Tony asked.

"Nothing, now that you mention it," Amy said. "I'll miss you too. But we'll have next summer; and the summer after that we'll both be finished."

"And sent to work in the salt mines. We could be miles apart."

"We might not. And you'll have our own car by then and if I can find a good job I may be motorised too. In the meantime we can write and send photographs. Do you have a scanner for sending photographs by e-mail?"

"I can get one. Amy, when we've done our two years' hard labour—"

"Then we can talk about it," she said firmly. She had sometimes daydreamed about a permanent relationship with Tony but it was only a daydream. Tony might be

Mr Right but, on the other hand, he might turn out to be Mr Definitely Wrong. All the same, he was a friend. Her very best friend.

Tony, clearly, had it in mind to be more than a friend. He had been holding her lightly by the waist but now, as he kissed her, his hands strayed. Amy broke off the kiss and moved quickly to trap his hands under her armpits.

"Now what's wrong?" Tony asked.

"You know very well. I don't want to be unkind. If it hurts you to play by my rules, let's go inside."

Tony recovered his hands and returned them to her waist. Amy relaxed. "There was an article in one of those intellectual magazines," Tony said huskily. "According to the writer, half of the world's social problems would be cured if men understood that the average woman needs a long, slow foreplay and if women realised the enormous pressure the average man suffers from his hormones."

"He may be right," Amy admitted. "You remember the first bit and I'll try to bear the rest of it in mind."

"The point is that if you'd go with the flow you might realise that something wonderful was waiting to happen."

"All things are possible. But for now, Tony, I'm still not ready to get into a major relationship."

"But if you were, it would be with me?"

"Very probably." Amy recalled her father's advice. "Almost certainly."

"Then when you are ready . . . ?"

"No promises," Amy said firmly. "For now, I can only say that I'm not yet ready. I think one would have to love somebody very much to want to do anything so damn silly with them. I dare say it's all right in practice. Most people seem to enjoy it. But I'm not ripe for it and for all the emotional upheavals that would follow and I don't want it. Not yet. I can do without the distraction. Please understand, Tony."

Tony ran his hand up her back and rubbed the back of her neck in the way which he knew she enjoyed. "I think I do understand. And it's all right, Amy. Just you remember, when you feel that you're ready, that there's somebody who wants you desperately."

"I'll remember," Amy said. "That's a very nice thing to say. The nicest thing anybody ever said to me. But it's still no go." She put her arms round his neck and they kissed. His hands moved to clasp her buttocks to pull her hard against him and she let them remain there. She felt that she was following her father's advice. Another first.

Inside a large Christmas card showing a Vermont snow scene, Tony wrote in his untidy handwriting:

> Getting on great, most of business management is common sense, a doddle. You should see the gliders here, got all the whistles and bells. Joined a club near Cambridge, Mass. Tell you one thing, though. Thought at first things are cheaper here or the rate of exchange is good, then on study of wages and profit margins realised we're being ripped off in Britain. Guess I'd better get on the side of the rippers-off, not the rippees, but there's margin for a bit of streamlining. Value for money

makes money. (As do the cheapest and the very best.)

May not be able to see you this summer, Mum marrying third husband, insists I'm there for moral support. Got to go, I'm well remembered in her will and prefer stay that way. If I can snatch a few days post-wedding, I'll be with you.

Tony managed to return to Britain that summer, only to be gathered up by his father and swept off on a lightning tour of his business enterprises. During the autumn, he e-mailed to Amy:

Desperately saddened didn't make it. Spent the few days pretending appreciate incomprehensible machinery. Don't need to know how machinery works, important thing is how much it cost and what it can do and when time to replace. Balance sheets made more sense. Pointed out a few accounting fallacies, so in good books.

After I finish here, Dad has promised me a year free to see if I can make it as a writer. That's what I want most of all. I *know* I can write. God! If I could only get one book published, just one, see myself in print, I'd go and work for Dad for the rest of my life and be content to write in spare time. There's got to be plenty plots in Big Business surely? Also Dad dangles a special carrot – my own glider if I finish with flying colours. Worth sweating for? He's set a high target but I can meet it with minimum effort. Business Studies come easy to me.

Eight months and several letters later Amy wrote by e-mail:

> Congrats exam results. See you soon? You're not only one has future planned by eager parent. Dad attended my graduation, then took me nearest hotel and bought me large drink . . .

Mr Fergusson had settled Amy with a large gin-and-tonic in a too-low armchair in the corner of the almost empty lounge. He raised a rather smaller malt whisky in salute. "This isn't just a celebration," he said. "I have something to tell you—"

"If it's about the birds and bees," Amy said, "I've read a book."

Mr Fergusson laughed but refused to digress. "I would hope so too. No, this is more important than mere sex. I've had an offer – a very good one, financially. It's been on what they call the back burner for a while and I've kept it quiet until now rather than distract you from your degree exams, but I can't put off much longer. It would mean going abroad for a year or so, to set up a met. station and forecasting service in one of the oil-rich Arab countries. I want to do it very much. It would set us up nicely."

"But what about the business here?"

Mr Fergusson nodded. "There's the rub. I've worked a long time to build up a solid client list and I'm not going to sacrifice it for the sake of a single contract. That's where you come in."

"Me?" Amy said.

He showed a moment's irritation. How could someone so slow in the uptake have managed a physics degree? "Who else?" he demanded. "Good Lord, here you are, knowing more about my methods than anybody else in the world, with a brand-new degree but in much need of a job at long last," he took a deep breath, "and here I am, offering you what amounts to a partnership and a chance to take over the whole shebang when I retire and all you'd have to do is to keep the business side of it running – send out accounts and bank the money – and fax me the Met Office figures whenever they come in and disseminate what I send back. You could do all that, couldn't you?"

"Yes," said Amy. "But—"

"No buts. And you know quite enough to answer any urgent queries as they come in. No need to stress the fact that I'm several thousand miles away. That's all there is to it. I'll pay you a salary and cover the household expenses. What do you say?"

Amy considered for a few moments. She had half expected to make tea at the Air Ministry for years before getting such a chance. Even so, there might still be room for a little negotiating. "It doesn't leave much margin for days off."

"Do what I do. Choose a settled period and forecast a day or two ahead. You can use your laptop from almost anywhere. If you check occasionally, you should spot any sudden changes before they become imminent."

"Could I use your car while you're away?" she asked.

"No problem. It's insured for you anyway, at colossal expense."

"And your glider?" He hesitated. "You let me use it before," she pointed out.

"But I was there."

"You were on the ground. If I'd got into difficulties, you wouldn't have been there to solve my problems for me."

"I suppose it'll be all right," he said at last. "But you're responsible for maintenance. And be careful with it. It's only insured third-party, fire and theft. Comprehensive insurance on a glider comes a bit heavy."

"You'll be able to afford the latest and the best when you come back," Amy pointed out. "Can I charge my aerotow fees to you? Or shall we start serious negotiations about my salary?"

"I'll go that far," said her father reluctantly. "But if you start talking about pension rights and maternity leave, the deal's off. Well, what do you think?"

"You've just hired yourself a partner and business manager." They shook hands.

Ten days later, Mr Fergusson flew out from Gatwick. At the last hour, they both showed signs of developing cold feet but each, in seeking to reassure the other, calmed their own fears.

As they waited in the airport lounge for his flight to be called, Mr Fergusson conceived a new worry. "Young Tony's due back soon, isn't he?"

"Early next month."

"I don't want the two of you staying in the house together while I'm away. That would not be a good idea."

Amy laughed. "I know. He's going to stay at the Hall.

They're opening up a few rooms to make an apartment for him. Tony's father has something in mind for the longer term. Anyway, there's nothing like that, not really. Tony's the brother I never had."

Mr Fergusson could well remember that, by definition, there are two sides to any relationship. "But are you the sister he never had?" he asked.

"Well, no," Amy said. "Not exactly."

"But you can cope?"

"Don't worry, I'm being very careful."

Mr Fergusson boarded his plane wearing a thoughtful expression but looking forward to the new challenge. He was over the Mediterranean before it occurred to him that there might be an alternative meaning to Amy's words. He could only hope that she would go on being careful. One of his reasons for jumping at the lucrative new contract was in the expectation of having to fund a wedding, preferably of the white variety. Insurance policy or no, he was determined to do well by Amy.

Amy, piloting her father's car very carefully homeward along the motorways, was still nervous. It had looked so easy when her father had been doing most of it but she could now begin to imagine all sorts of uncertainties. What had he forgotten to tell her? Suppose he returned to a business which had lost all its clients? Suppose she even failed to predict a major storm? There could be loss of life, prosecution, lawsuits.

She arrived home without accident, which she regarded as a good omen. Perhaps she would manage after all.

The job turned out to be as simple as her father had

promised. It seemed almost a shame to take the money. Even on days when telephone lines to the Middle East were unavailable for their faxes or when the pressures of his contract prevented him from replying promptly, she could cope. As her father had remarked years earlier, she had an unusual facility for visualising the invisible. Air movements triggered by different temperatures and influenced by the movement of the earth and the latent energy of humidity, these made sense to her while others might struggle for understanding. Aided by her father's very sophisticated computer program, she put out the various local forecasts demanded by the clients and answered their urgent questions. In the main it meant a flurry of activity in the early mornings and a second burst of activity in late afternoon when the forecasts for the chain of local morning papers were prepared and faxed out.

After a few weeks of the new regime, Tony returned. Somewhere during his travels he had acquired a veneer of synthetic confidence to cloak his sexual shyness. As a result, their first day together again might have been the last.

Amy met Tony off the plane at Gatwick. He was his old self in the car except for an apparently accidental pat on her thigh. When they reached the Hall he took her to explore his new flat. The smaller rooms on the ground floor had been decorated by someone with taste and furnished with suitable pieces from the house. There were three bedrooms and one of them, Amy noted, would make a suitable nursery with easy access to a lawn.

It was just as she decided that this was not likely to be

a factor in the equation that he moved in on her. Clearly he had decided to be masterful, expecting her to yield. Amy, for her part, decided to do no such thing. She had had some experience of fighting off forceful suitors during her time at university, so she bit his tongue and slapped his crotch and then pushed him over the coffee table so that he fell with a thump.

He picked himself up tenderly and moved to a deep settee. "You didn't have to half-kill me," he said. "I can take a hint."

"But you weren't taking hints," Amy said. "And you weren't taking no for an answer."

He looked properly ashamed of himself. "All right. I got carried away. It was the excitement of seeing you again after all this time. You can't believe how I've missed you. I'm sorry, Amy." He patted the seat beside him. "Come and sit down and say that you forgive me."

"No more rough stuff?"

"Definitely not."

"All right. But I'm not in the mood for wrestling."

She settled beside him and he put an arm loosely around her shoulders as he had done many times in the past. With her father's warning in mind she hesitated to add to any feeling of rejection that he might have, so she let the arm remain – for the moment.

"Am I forgiven?" he asked.

"Just about," she said. "Bear in mind, nobody loves a rapist."

"I have a lot to learn about girls," he said. "Will you tell me something?"

"What?"

He was silent for a full minute. "Just suppose something. You meet a handsome man, beautifully groomed—"

"You?" Amy asked.

"No, somebody much better looking than me. He's tall and he has a sexy foreign accent. He tells you that he loves you. He says that you're beautiful. All right so far?"

"So far," Amy said, "I like it."

"He kisses you, artistically. Then, suddenly, he produces silk scarves and gently but firmly ties you up. Still murmuring words of love, he starts to kiss every inch of your body, working his way down—"

Amy leaped to her feet. "Stop it! You're just trying to get me going."

He sighed and got to his feet. "All right," he said. "You can't blame me for trying. I just wanted to find out how we stood."

"We stand just as we did before you went abroad."

He clasped his hands behind his back and approached her. "Before I went abroad, you wouldn't grudge me the comfort of one little kiss."

Amy gave him one little kiss and stepped back. "Anyway," she said, "if he was going to kiss every inch of my body he'd have to get my clothes off first and I don't see how he was going to do that with my hands and feet tied. You don't think your fantasies through." She left quickly and hurried home to the empty house.

He came to Firhaven next morning in a suitably chastened mood and soon it was as if they had never been apart. For several hours on most days, while Amy was attending to the forecasting service, Tony absented himself and it was understood that he was in his father's study and making steady use of his word processor. The remainder of each day he spent with Amy, even helping out with the book-keeping and accounts. He wrote several computer programs to simplify the business side of the consultancy.

As often as they could, they went gliding. At first, they both used Mr Fergusson's glider. Tony had placed an order for the latest and best but he was apprehensive. "Dad said 'Go ahead and order what you want'," he told Amy. "I don't suppose he realised how much a top-of-the-range glider, fully equipped, can cost, but a promise is a promise." Mr Hope-Williams, however, was proud of his first-born and appreciated the work which had gone into his qualification from the Harvard School of Business. He accepted the cost without demur. When the new glider arrived, Amy, after an explanatory talk from Mr Cardinal and a much longer one from Tony, was allowed to make several flights in it, exploring the glider's climb and glide performance. Some day, she told herself, she too would aspire to the latest and the best.

Mr Fergusson sent Amy an irritable fax:

I've just had my credit card account including payments to the club for your aerotows. We can't afford it. You're mad. You must be going up and down like a yo-yo. For God's sake, when you go up, stay up for a decent flight. Have you lost the knack or something?

Amy replied:

I'm working towards my FAI silver badge. Tony got his while he was in the States. I have to come down at regular intervals to check that there aren't any new faxes in. Don't worry about it. If you like, I'll pay my own launches. As business manager I can award myself a salary increase to make this possible. Remember, I know exactly how much is coming in and I think I'm worth much more than I'm paying myself. What's more, I'm thinking of auditing your expenses.

No more was heard from Mr Fergusson on that subject.

Amy had no difficulty achieving the 50km distance flight and the height gain of 1,000 metres required by the *Federation Aeronautique Internationale* for their silver medal, but the sustained flight of not less than five hours evaded her until Tony allowed her to use his new glider for the purpose. The loan coincided with ideal conditions and she was still soaring, high above the clouds, some while after the five hours had passed when Tony contacted her on his radio to demand her return to earth. "Come in Number Seven," said his voice. "Your time is up." She half expected Tony to require some *quid pro quo* for his generosity, but he endeared himself by being the same affectionate and reliable if sometimes conceited friend. Amy was surprised and, if not quite insulted, at least a little piqued. There had been passing occasions during Tony's absence when she had almost decided to give in to his importunities and if he had made his first approach more subtly . . . well, who knows?

*   *   *

It was a dank and misty autumn, but on one golden day when the leaves and berries were bright in the sun, Amy was awaiting her turn on the Flying List for the tow-plane when Mr Cardinal, who had been standing in as Launch Point Controller but had just been relieved, approached her. He asked after her father's activities abroad and her own efforts and then said, "You're both keeping well?"

Amy thought that his mind seemed to be elsewhere. "We're fine," she said. "Dad's pleased with his progress. You seem to be walking stiffly."

He shrugged. "*Anno domini*, coupled with a lot of standing around. Let's hobble as far as the seat." The breeze had come in from the opposite direction to the prevailing wind so that the launch point was now opposite the seat, although this was set back some distance from the runway for reasons of safety. When he had settled with a grunt of relief he resumed, "You remember our talk about Shakespeare?"

"Of course. And I remember that you said that you'd speak to me again about it."

He smiled but lowered his voice. "Now is the hour. How would you like to be Shakespeare to my Christopher Marlowe?"

Amy looked at him blankly. She had been reading the biographies of Shakespeare and Marlowe and felt prepared for an academic discussion. "I don't understand."

He looked up, watching a glider slide overhead. He was looking older, she thought. "I'll explain. I don't think that I'll ever write again in my old style. I've said all that I've got to say and I'm too old and indolent to go chasing all over the globe researching my backgrounds. So no more hairy-chested yarns about big men fighting the odds and each other and adventuring all over the globe."

"Your books will be missed," Amy said.

He glanced at her but saw that she was perfectly sincere. "Thank you. I've been working on one last book which is quite different. It's about people rather than deeds. I suppose that you could call it a love story. It's so different from my previous books that I don't even want to have it published under my name. I wouldn't want it compared with what went before and I don't want my readers to think that I went soft. I really couldn't face up to the hoo-ha of being interviewed and reviewed and doing signings and all the razzmatazz that usually goes with my books. And I want to leave my reputation as it stands, not clouded by the record of something quite different, something which may even be a total flop. A novel may not be autobiographical but you put a lot of yourself into it. My first venture into writing was like taking off my clothes on stage." He produced his old, shy smile and again looked years younger. "Perhaps I'd have had the figure for it in those days but not any longer, so I don't think that I could go through it all again. Can you understand that?"

Amy tried to imagine her words being offered for approval to a vast readership and decided that excitement might well be balanced by trepidation. "Yes," she said thoughtfully. "I believe I can."

"So I'm looking for somebody who would be prepared to be my front, have their name on the cover and their picture on the back flap, and do the signings and interviews if it goes that far."

"Wow!" said Amy.

Mr Cardinal mistook her surprise for reluctance. "I can make it worth your while," he said. "For a start, you could keep the Public Lending Rights, because I'm already far over the limit and wouldn't have earned any more anyway. You'd pay the tax on the remainder and we'd split what's left down the middle. You might have a nice little earner for years. Or, of course, you might not. If not, you wouldn't have lost anything."

"I suppose not. But would anyone really believe that I'd written it?"

"Yes, I think they would. The story looks at the world through the eyes of a woman, so it's the sort of novel that would be more likely to come from the pen of a young woman than an old man. You would know, from instinct or experience, what for me has been the accumulated observation of fifty years and a little more recent research." He chuckled suddenly. "I've been asking the ladies of my acquaintance some very strange questions. Most of them were surprisingly forthcoming but one or two thought that I was – what's the current expression – *coming on* to them."

Amy sighed in relief. At last Mrs Hogweed's insinuations were explained. She moved closer along the bench. She had very little idea as to what a novel might earn. Without Derek Cardinal's name on the cover, she thought, its sales might be limited. But the idea of a little extra income to herself was very attractive. She hunted for snags. "What if you walk under a bus or something?" she asked.

He shrugged. "Then you may as well keep the lot.

Frankly, I'm not worried about the money. I'll never spend what I've saved and I've no close relatives waiting to inherit. I've made large bequests to charities but it's not easy to know which make best use of their money and which ones waste most of it in salaries and publicity. By the time the tax officials finish with my estate, there wouldn't be much left of any last-minute extras."

The Launch Point Controller was beckoning to her and two members were waiting to help push the glider out. "It sounds attractive," she said uncertainly. "Can we talk later?"

She got up but he rose with her and they walked towards the glider. Courtesy required her to walk at his slower pace. The tow-plane was taxiing into position.

"I wouldn't expect you to go into it blind," he said. "I have the top copy in my car. Collect it from me before you go. Read it and return it. Will you be here on Friday?"

"Almost certainly," Amy said. She reached the glider and settled in the cockpit.

"Let me have it back then with your final answer." He started to say something else, but Amy had closed the canopy. By the time she had fastened the numerous straps the cable was attached and the Launch Point Controller was glaring at her. During the flight she remembered to keep a sharp lookout but part of her mind was dallying with the thought of perhaps being able to afford a glider as good as Tony's. Some clothes. Perhaps even one or two items of jewellery, not too expensive. Failing which, surely it would run to a small, second-hand car.

A succession of lows brought unsettled, wet and windy

weather so that for the next few days Amy was busy relaying warnings to sports clubs, fair organisers and yachtsmen. Between times, she and Tony carried out some essential glider maintenance in the club's hangar. With a sudden pang of guilt she realised on the Thursday evening that she had still not looked at Mr Cardinal's typescript.

She fetched it from the back seat of her father's car, where it had languished for half the week, and settled down in front of an open fire. But it was a long book, too long to swallow at one or even two sittings. Amy compromised. She read the opening pages, dipped into the body at two or three points and then carefully read the last chapter which, in her experience, was where the essence of a book was likely to be found. It seemed to be, as he had said, a love story – told with all the charm and poetic imagery of his other style but with a new attention to the inner workings of emotion so delicate that coming to the last words was like emerging from a real experience.

The Friday was another fine day but foul weather was again approaching from the Atlantic. She was therefore not disposed to linger and chat with Mr Cardinal when they met in the clubhouse. "It's a beautiful ending," she said, handing him back the bulky parcel.

"I thought so too," he said. He waited for her to say more but she had exhausted her comments. "You'll do it then?" he asked.

"I suppose so."

He beamed at her. "Excellent! Now remember, this arrangement is a secret between ourselves and nobody else. Promise?"

"Absolutely."

"I'll pass it to my agent on your behalf. Is that all right?"

"Perfectly," she said. "Now, please excuse me if I dash off. I want to get a flight before the weather breaks again."

Once launched, she found the perfect thermal and forgot about Mr Cardinal and books and everything else except for the sheer joy of sailing the sky.

She was reminded of their agreement occasionally during the succeeding months, by demands for her signature on a contract, for a photograph and for a potted biography. Any editorial queries were answered on her behalf by Derek Cardinal and he also undertook to deal with such matters as proof-reading. She was brought up short, however, when the first instalment of the advance against royalties reached her. Surely young authors were not always advanced such sums? It was probably a mistake and they would want most of it back. Also, there would be tax to pay. She consulted an accountant, who was able to put a figure on the probable tax liability. She opened a new savings account and banked the cheque, keeping back only a modest portion for her own immediate use and sending Derek Cardinal a cheque for half the estimated balance after tax. When this produced no amazed response she began to believe that it might be real money after all.

Her one concern about the loan of her identity centred on Tony. She took her promise to Derek Cardinal seriously. If the book ever came out – a concept which still seemed quite incredible to her – and if he found out about it, Tony might believe that she had once again stolen his thunder. He might be hurt. On the other hand, it would surely be a passing wonder which she might be able to hide from him. The publication of new novels was only rarely forced on her attention and then only by the television when the author was famous or notorious for some other activity. At a pinch, she might soothe Tony's ruffled feelings and restore his male pride by capitulating to his occasionally renewed pleas and make love with him. It would, she knew, happen some day.

It came, therefore, as a shock when, during the following summer, she received from the publishers an invitation, almost a summons, to attend a publication-day party during the next month to publicise the new book. She would be expected to sign copies, be interviewed, shake hands and say a few words. Negotiations were in hand for TV cameras to attend.

Suddenly the impersonation became a reality. Derek Cardinal was not to be seen around the gliding club, nor was there any answer on his phone. A panic message left on his answering machine failed to provoke a return call. He was believed to be lecturing to a summer school somewhere vaguely in the north but there was also word in the club that he had been unwell.

For several days she went around in mental turmoil. The deception was about to blow up in her face. Her father was due back in Britain before publication day, but she was not worried about his reaction. He had always considered that nothing was beyond her capability and he would accept her accomplishment with quiet pride. Tony, however, had been increasingly despondent about his writing and his year of grace was running out. If she attended the party there was bound to be something in the papers – that was surely the whole objective. They might even print her picture. Everyone would see it. *Tony* would see it. She would then be in the position of having pipped him at the post once again and he would never forgive her.

At the height of her unease, a possible solution was presented to her. A notice in the club-house reminded her, if she had ever absorbed the information in the first place, that the National Soaring Championships were to be held in Aberdeenshire during a week which conveniently included the date of the party. The Scottish papers would surely not review a book by an unknown English girl. By the time they returned, the fuss and nonsense would be over and if Tony ever happened on a copy in a bookshop she might be able to pass it off as being by someone of similar name and coincidentally similar appearance. Or by then he might himself be a published author and able to surmount the blow to his dignity.

Tony, when consulted about attending the Championships, at first showed reluctance on the grounds that he needed the few remaining weeks of his sabbatical in the hope of writing something worthy of the consecration of print.

But his attendance in Scotland, or at least his absence from his usual haunts and sources of information, was essential. Even in her absence the publication day ballyhoo might go ahead. "You couldn't write much of a book in a week," Amy pointed out. "And you might even pick up some material to write about. A magazine article about the Championships would at least get you started."

Tony would have none of it. "I want to be an author, not a journalist."

Amy was suddenly inspired. "If you're going to sit in your ivory tower, writing like mad, you won't be using your glider. Will you lend it to me? It's much more suitable. I'd have a better chance of coming back with a few trophies to show you . . ."

Tony's reaction to this suggestion was inspired more by the mention of trophies than by fear of damage to his precious glider. "Perhaps you're right," he said. "A week might be neither here nor there. And a change of scene might be just what I need before putting my nose to the grindstone. We'll both go."

Amy faxed her father:

Will you definitely be home as promised? I am long overdue for a holiday (Annual Leave Entitlement, it's called) and Tony and I want to attend the Nat Champs in Scotland. And can I borrow your glider and trailer and car for that week? Believe it or not, for that week only I can pay my own petrol and hotels and entry fees and aerotows, having been very thrifty in your absence.

Mr Fergusson replied:

I will be home as planned. The job is finished and I am only crossing the eyes and dotting the teas, training staff and persuading neighbouring states to furnish data in return for a share of the forecasts. You've done very well (to judge from the letters

113

of appreciation you've carefully included among the faxes. How many letters of complaint you've held back I'll probably never know.) I was rather looking forward to doing a little gliding on my return – couldn't you share with Tony? Otherwise I'll be reduced to spending my leisure winning the garden back from the cannibals, who have no doubt taken it over while I've been away. But I suppose a week can be spared. You've earned it. Just be careful with my favourite toy.

Amy wrote a polite letter to the publishers, explaining that due to inescapable commitments she would be abroad at the time of publication and for an unspecified period on either side. (She was telling the truth as she saw it. In her mind, Scotland was 'abroad'.) She added her good wishes and promised to sign books on some other occasion.

Then she got down to such urgent tasks as rescuing the garden and, with Tony, bringing the two gliders back as close to a state of perfection as was possible. Amy's original proposal had been that they would share Tony's glider, but at that point he had dug in his heels. After taking more than a week off from his writing and having towed a glider much of the length of Britain, he said, he wanted to cram as many competitive flights as he could into the time available.

Mr Fergusson arrived back at Gatwick only four or five hours late. Amy, who had kept in touch with the plane's progress by telephone, got caught in traffic and only just arrived in time to meet him.

"You look very bronzed and fit," she said as they wheeled his trolley to the car park.

"I probably look a hundred years old. It's been hard work in a way, but rewarding. Financially, I mean. And every penny of it free of tax."

"Was it difficult?"

"Not really. Apart from military spin-offs, they really only want to know two things – when will the rains come and is there danger of locust weather?"

He allowed Amy to drive him home. He desperately wanted to ask how things stood between herself and Tony but he was sure that a direct question would be met by resistance or evasion. He decided to approach obliquely. "How's Tony getting along?" he asked as they pulled out of the car park.

"He did very well in his exams, but I think I told you that. If you mean his writing, he's depressed. I've seen some of his attempts. He uses words well but his ideas about plots are too trivial to put him in with a chance."

"And his time's running out? He needs to put his writing away until he's lived a little, watched how people act and listened to how they speak. Is he going to work for his father?"

Amy put off answering until she had negotiated a difficult roundabout. "That's the general idea," she said.

"You'll miss him."

"He'll still be next door. Mr Hope-Williams wants to set up an office to integrate his various businesses financially and Tony's to take charge of it. I think he'll do it well. He says that the profitability of each of the businesses depends to some extent on what oncosts are charged against it for central services like transport and the shareholders scream bloody murder if they feel hard done by. And the office is to be housed at the Hall. They're making some internal alterations now, including making a self-contained flat for Tony."

"You didn't tell me any of this in your faxes."

Amy sighed. "The first thing you'd have wanted to know would have been how big the flat was – whether it was big enough for a family."

That was exactly the first question which had leaped to Mr Fergusson's mind, so he denied it indignantly. "I'm more concerned about increased traffic and the effect on property prices," he said.

"The effect on property values will be a damn sight less than if the place was sold and bungalows built in the grounds," Amy pointed out. "Anyway there will only be a handful of accountancy staff and a computer programmer. Not exactly rush-hour traffic."

Now that the subject had been broached, Mr Fergusson felt free to pursue it. "Are you pleased that Tony will still be next door?" he asked.

"Yes, you old romantic. I'm pleased. Tony's a very good friend. We get along great. I took your advice and I've been doing what I can to bolster his confidence." She paused while her parent shifted uneasily in his seat. "Within reason. We're not sleeping together if that's what's worrying you. Never have and probably never will."

It was Mr Fergusson's turn to sigh. "I always hoped that you two would make a go of it."

"I dare say you did," Amy said tartly. "But we're not

116

going to re-arrange our lives to take account of what you always hoped. If it happens, it happens. If not, forget it. Tony will have to grow up a bit and lose some of his cockiness before . . . before anything."

Mr Fergusson lapsed into thoughtful silence for the rest of the journey.

When he had recovered from jet-lag and general exhaustion he was pleased to find that the house, garden and business were as orderly as he had been led to believe.

He saw the two equipages away, very early one morning a week later. "I would dearly have loved to come with you," he said, "but somebody has to mind the shop. The trouble with being a one man band is that you're shackled."

"Did you think I hadn't noticed?" Amy asked absently. She was checking that the essential tools were aboard. "But I'll be back in about ten days and then I'll take a share of the load. We can take it in turns to go away and recover."

"I hope so. I'm not far off retirement age and I'd like to start taking it a little easier."

"You mean you want to put your feet up while I work to pay you a pension?"

"I'm glad you thought of that idea," he said. He stepped back and waved until the little convoy was out of sight. Then he went back to bed.

Sustained by sandwiches and thermos flasks, they did the run in a single day. Tony was driving one of his father's Range Rovers while Amy had her father's more modest and less powerful saloon; but Tony had the more modern, and therefore lighter, glider and trailer. At the end of the first hour, Tony led the way into a motorway services where they exchanged burdens, remembering at the last moment to switch trailer number-plates. After that they could cruise the motorways at or slightly above the legal limit. In the crowded Midlands they found themselves getting held up by slower vehicles and unable to slot the long trailers into the faster traffic, so they took to hogging one of the middle lanes.

They crossed the Border in early afternoon and Amy, who had seen Scotland often on the weather maps but had not appreciated its scale, thought that their journey must be almost over. But Scotland, she discovered, seemed to go on for ever. The bald mountains of the Borders gave way to scenery much like what they had left at home, but it was noticeably cooler. The older buildings, Amy noticed, were mostly of stone, with higher, narrowed windows and less overhangs to catch the wind.

Motorways gave way to dual carriageways and at last to country roads where the long trailers had to be nursed carefully through the traffic. The mountains of the Highlands showed ahead. As an alternative to routes which would have taken them through streets and urban traffic they had opted for one of two climbs over passes. Late in the evening they found the small hotel where they had booked two rooms.

In the morning, much restored by country breakfasts and a great deal of coffee, they towed the trailers to the airstrip. It was Sunday, the day before the competitions were to begin. They checked in at the clubhouse and showed their logbooks to the Chief Flying Instructor. As a necessary formality, each then went up with the CFI for a check flight in a club two-seater, after which, working cheerfully together, they soon had the two gliders unloaded and rigged, the joints neatly taped to prevent unnecessary drag and the controls and instruments checked. Around them one or two other gliders were being rigged and there were several in the air.

By mid-afternoon, the work was done. Tony straightened his back and looked around, taking in the scenery for the first time. They were in flat farmland, the bottom of a shallow valley, but to the west the flanking hills grew into the mountains of the Scottish Highlands and the silver birches gave way to conifers. It was a tranquil scene and one to delight the heart of a romantic, but Tony's mind was not on the scenery.

"Looks like good gliding," he said. "Let's go up and get an idea of the geography."

Amy was stiff and tired. The wings are not assembled to gliders without a lot of bodily contortions. "We got a pretty good idea of the geography from the site briefing the CFI gave us."

"Looking at maps and charts isn't the same as seeing the ground and feeling the air movement." Tony looked at the leisurely activity around them. "I'd expected a lot more hustle and bustle. Most of these seem to be locals. I'd expected more of a turnout for the Championships."

"Only fourteen entries registered so far in our class, they were saying."

"I reckon I've got a good chance of some results," Tony said thoughtfully.

Amy noticed the use of the first person singular but decided to ignore it in the interest of harmony. "You should pick up a prize or two," she assured him. "So far, I haven't seen any better machines."

She spoke in innocence, but Tony lifted his chin. "You wouldn't be suggesting that it'll be down to the glider, not to me?"

Amy decided that tiredness and pre-competition nerves were talking, so she bit back an answer which would have put the cat well among the pigeons. "I didn't say that at all."

"You implied it."

"Well, if I did, I didn't mean to." This was as close to an apology as Amy had any intention of giving.

Tony was not going to be put off. "Flying identical gliders, do you really think you could beat me?"

Amy's pride was also at stake, but she was still prepared for compromise. "That's a big question," she said. "You're becoming very good but you don't always appreciate the effects of the wind and the weather."

"You're evading the question."

"The question doesn't arise."

Tony's mouth tightened. "It can be—" He stopped, unsure what verb to use. Raise? Arouse? Amy would certainly pounce on any grammatical absurdities. He tried to relax. "I'll tell you what we'll do," he said. "I'll take your glider up now and you can take mine. We'll aerotow to two thousand feet and release over the airstrip. You can set the course. We'll time each other from release to touchdown and I'll bet you I get round quicker. There!"

Amy had had enough. "You're on," she said. "I studied

the map in the clubhouse. There are two small lochs not far to the west of here. The CFI mentioned them in his briefing. Round those and back, but starting from one thousand feet, not two. Right?"

Tony should have been warned by the last stipulation but in his chagrin he had stopped thinking clearly. "Right," he said.

"What are the stakes?"

"If I win, you have to sleep with me."

"And if you lose?"

Tony smirked. "I have to sleep with you."

Amy might even have accepted the wager if Tony had been her dear friend of the previous decade and the bet had been made among their usual giggles and snorts of laughter. Although it was going to happen some day, it would be with the real Tony and not with this jealous stranger, occasionally glimpsed over the years but never liked. Tony, she decided, was due to be taken down a peg or two. She knew his weaknesses and she had chosen the course with those in mind. If he could beat her over it in the older glider and starting from a launch at reduced height, then pigs – other pigs than Tony – could fly. "In your dreams," she said briskly.

Tony's face hardened. "All right," he said. "You set the stake. Anything you like."

"Loser does a streak at the next Gliding Club dinner-dance," she heard her own voice say. Once the words were out she nearly tried to call them back, but pride would not allow it. Anyway, if the unthinkable occurred she could invent some escape clause.

For a moment she thought Tony was going to break

down and laugh as so often in the past and the whole incident would have passed by. But the gleam of amusement died away. "Done!" he said quickly. "You want to go first?"

Whoever flew second might gain an advantage from the mistakes of the other, but Amy was not going to quibble over such details. "If you like," she said.

Three local club members helped her to push Tony's glider, backwards, to the launch point. There was only one glider ahead of her, no others waiting and two tow-planes working. Her turn came within a few minutes, almost before she had had time to mount her camera, fasten her straps and remind herself of the few differences in the controls. She saw Tony speaking with the pilot. The tow-line was attached. Tony came back to her. "One thousand feet over the airstrip," he said. "It's understood."

The Launch Point Controller signalled to the pilot that all was clear above and behind; then to take up slack and finally 'all out'. Moments later, they were airborne and she was committed. Above the airstrip and at 950 feet on the altimeter, to allow for instrument lag, Amy released the tow and banked round to the west. The glider handled sweetly and she adjusted the trim to suit her own weight.

Her choice of a lower than usual release height had been calculated. From two thousand feet it might have been possible for a modern glider to complete the course in a single glide, but from half that elevation it would definitely not. Somewhere along the way, height would have to be gained in rising air, but the breeze was light and a thin, even layer of high cloud suggested stable conditions with little lift. Tony's answer to such problems was usually to look for other gliders circling and glide to join them. But the other gliders were south and east.

On the outward, upwind leg, Amy managed to save a little height. She rounded the two lochs, giving them a wide berth, and gained a slight lift from the nearby hillside. She photographed the lochs with her 35mm camera to supplement the evidence of the Global Positioning Satellite that she had completed the course. She flew over the road, but the tarmac was not sending up an appreciable quantity of warm air.

A wisp of low cloud hung half a mile to the south, holding out a promise of a minor thermal. It went against the grain to turn off the shortest track and sacrifice height, but it was the best course. She fretted with anxiety as she flew, but under the cloud she found the rising air for which she had hoped. She spiralled upward for five minutes, gaining a thousand feet, and had enough height for a fast glide back to the airstrip. She flew a standard left-hand circuit, set the air-brake and flaps, lowered the single wheel of the undercarriage and touched down quickly, but as gently as a collector with a precious vase, clicking her stopwatch as she slowed to a halt. "Beat that, you bastard," she said aloud. And if he did summon up a miracle and beat it, she could always fulfil the terms of the bet with a paper bag over her head.

Tony came running and they compared watches. "Twenty-six minutes dead," Tony said.

"Twenty-five forty-three," Amy said, "but if you need

123

to snatch every advantage, I'll give you the benefit. Your turn."

The drill was repeated with the other glider. When Tony released over the airstrip, Amy was already in her father's car and making her way back to the road. By the time the cruciform shape of her father's glider came sliding across the sky, she was parked where she could overlook the two lochs.

Hampered by the less favourable gliding angle of the older design of glider, Tony arrived lower and he cut too close to the water in an attempt to save both time and distance. The air over the cold water was sinking and he banked away for the nearby hill where the breeze climbing the slope gave him some lift. He had to track to and fro several times to gain the height he needed before setting off back towards the airstrip, taking what advantage he could of every fold in the ground.

Amy turned the car and headed back east, trying to keep the glider in sight without taking her attention off the road. Derek Cardinal had quoted a seventeenth-century proverb to her – 'The longest way round is the nearest way home'. On the face of it a seeming nonsense, but was it true in this instance? Her digression in search of a thermal had cost her time. Tony was making better speed than she had expected.

She turned off through the gates, looked at her watch and pulled a face. If Tony made it back to the airstrip it would probably not be within the time she had set; and if he ran out of lift and had to land in a field it would give her great satisfaction to bring his trailer to him and to remind him of the terms of their bet. But it was going to be close. Watch in hand, she left the car and ran.

Circumstances for the moment seemed to favour Tony. The breeze had picked up and he was getting a good lift from the rising slope, enough to keep him up and heading for the airstrip. His airspeed was not high, but he did not have to recover the time that Amy had spent in pursuit of her thermal. He struggled back with very little height in hand, came in low and made to turn upwind for his landing.

Amy's stopwatch passed the twenty-six minutes and she did a little tap-dance in the grass. The dinner-dancers would be favoured with a glimpse of Tony's manly charms and not her own slender body.

But in his refusal either to 'land out' or to waste precious time in gaining more height on the nearest suitable hillside, Tony had made the classic glider pilot's mistake of arriving low and slow. The slight wind gradient suddenly reduced his airspeed. The glider's nose dropped and he stalled the last six feet. There were ominous noises.

Six

Amy was among the first to reach the damaged glider but the Launch Point Controller, a military-looking man with silver hair and moustache and the beginning of an imposing stomach, was before her and several sets of feet came thumping over the grass on her heels. The prevalent reaction seemed to be relief that Tony was unhurt.

Amy was much more concerned about the glider. A medley of ill-assorted thoughts were jumbled in her mind. If her preliminary and rough calculations were correct and she really did get to keep half of the advance on Mr Cardinal's book after tax, she could well afford to buy her father at least one brand new glider complete with SatNav, radio and what Tony had called 'all the whistles and bells', but that was beside the point. She was entered in competition the very next day. She had spent the whole of an almost endless day hauling the long trailer north and she had laboured to dismantle and re-rig the glider, hauling it in and out of the trailer, and all, perhaps, for nothing. And she would have the same purgatory to undergo to get the damaged remains home again. Also, the glider had been her father's ewe lamb.

He had cherished it for years, taken it home to work on during the worst months of the year and written articles about it for *Gliding Monthly*. He talked to it. She suspected that he sang to it whenever she was out of earshot. When Amy's mother had been killed he had divided her share of his affection between his glider and Amy, in what proportion she had never dared to guess. Worst of all, Tony had done the damage in the hope of committing her to doing a streak at the dinner-dance. The fact that she herself had suggested that particular stake for the moment escaped her mind.

Amy seethed. "What have you *done*?" she cried.

Tony completed his climb out and tested his legs. "I didn't do anything," he said defiantly. "Your old glider let me down. Anyway, I was only knee-high. I think it's all right."

"It is *not* all right," Amy said. Looking at the glider, she was sure that there was a difference to the shape although she could not have put her finger on exactly where the difference lay. "And you came down from higher than my head. I heard something go. I can't fly it like this."

"You can't fly it at all until it has a fresh Certificate of Airworthiness," said the LPC firmly. "That was not just a bad landing, it was an accident. The procedure for notifying the CAA will have to be followed. Give me your Daily Inspection Book and I'll make an endorsement."

Tony stuck his jaw out. Amy thought that he was going to make things worse by arguing from an untenable position but he made a helpless gesture, conceding defeat. "I suppose it's insured," he muttered.

"Only the usual third party," she said. Even that, when

she came to think of it, was probably invalid because Tony had not been a named pilot, although she had more sense than to add further complications by mentioning that omission. "But that's not the point," she stormed. "I've hauled it all the way here in order to compete and now you've put me out before I've started. Well, we'll just have to share yours. You can have it Monday, Wednesday and Friday. I'll have it Tuesday and Thursday; and on Saturday we'll see who's still in the hunt."

Tony's face turned from red to white. "Oh come on!" he said. "I've towed all this way too. You can't ask me to give up half my days. I didn't *do* anything."

The growing throng around the glider had been joined by the Chief Flying Instructor along with other officials whose faces, in the heat of the moment, Amy failed to identify. She was just building up pressure, preparatory to an explosion of wrath, when she was spared the necessity. "Young man," the CFI said sternly, "you've just made the worst landing I've seen in years. You will come into the office, right now, to explain yourself. And I suggest that you jump at Miss . . . Miss Fergusson's offer. It's a very generous one. In her shoes I'd be demanding undisputed use of your glider for the whole week. Whether you will have any use for it yourself has yet to be decided."

The CFI and the men who by now Amy had recognised as the Club Secretary and the Competition Secretary set off back to the clubhouse with Tony trailing miserably in their wake. Amy looked round the other faces. "Now, who's going to help me unrig the glider and get it out of sight in its trailer before I break down and weep over it?"

Several pairs of hands were laid on the glider. There were new creaks from the structure as they trundled it backwards over the grass. It travelled slightly crabwise. The undercarriage had absorbed some of the impact by bending. Amy came in for a great deal of sympathy and not a little oblique flirtation, to which she was too miserable to respond.

Amy towed the trailer back to the hotel and parked it in the furthest corner of the rear car-park, where it would be out of sight and therefore as nearly as possible out of mind. Her morale was in urgent need of repair. She soothed herself with a warm bath and a change from her working jeans into a pretty dress, styled her hair and gave some attention to making up a face which she more usually left much as nature intended it. Thus restored, she felt strong enough to descend to the public areas of the hotel and she spent the early evening in the bar with one of her new admirers, drinking spritzers and talking gliding. Amy's admirer, a large young man with the slightly battered good looks of a rugby player and apparently unlimited funds, had a hoard of humorous and sometimes scurrilous stories about their fellow competitors.

Tony, very much shaken by his interview with the officials of the host club, had returned to the hotel and looked for Amy. The depth of his infamy had sunk in at last and had been rammed home by the attitudes of the other pilots. He wanted to apologise, to grovel, to offer her sole use of his glider, his body, his hand in marriage, his anything she might fancy, if she would only forgive and forget and go back to being the old Amy, his friend and confidante. But, finding her room empty, he looked into the bar and saw the two heads close together, laughing, and he knew that they were laughing at him, his ineptitude and his stupid behaviour. He went out instead for a long walk.

Amy phoned her father. She had wondered whether to withhold the news of the damaged glider until she returned, at which time she hoped that his joy in having his daughter home and working again might soften the blow. On the other hand, while there were some hundreds of miles between them seemed to be the ideal moment for confessing that she had allowed an imbecile to break his favourite toy. Mr Fergusson, who had been wondering how best to apprise Amy that he had come round to her view and intended to spend a significant part of his overseas earnings on a new glider, took the news with admirable restraint.

When Amy explained the deal she had struck with Tony, her father was cautious. "You should be all right on Tuesday," Mr Fergusson said. "Don't tell him yet but, if they let him fly at all, whether young Tony will get his second day's competition on Wednesday is open to question. There's a confused system of depressions coming across the Atlantic with fronts and occlusions in all directions. If it continued at the usual sort of pace – fifteen to twenty knots – it would have been with you early on Thursday, but it's showing signs of speeding up. The last one to follow an almost identical pattern caught all the forecasters out by arriving well ahead of time and bringing strong winds with it."

"So I may miss my turn on Thursday?"

"It may have gone through by then, or flattened out."

Mr Fergusson wished his daughter luck and went back with renewed zest to his study of the brochures for gliders at the very top of the range. Tony had relieved him of the need to make excuses for his planned extravagance. He liked the boy more and more, but he was damned if Tony would get within a mile of the glider which was smiling at him from the topmost brochure on the pile.

Tony returned from his walk in a mood which varied between shame and indignation. In his desperation to win his bet with Amy, he had made what at first he had considered to be a small error of judgement even if the consequences had been disproportionate. He quite accepted that he should not have made it. He had progressed beyond that standard. But there was no need for everybody to carry on as though he had peed against the club-house bar.

He was in time to see Amy part from her new friend. They would never be more than amusing company for each other, Amy knew. There had been no spark of sexual recognition between them, but for the moment he had helped to soothe her irritation. They laughed together at some last anecdote while Tony glowered across the room. Then, as the door closed behind her friend, she saw Tony. She hesitated for a moment, but Tony was Tony. He had shed his mutinous glower and she still had the glow of laughter in her mind. She smiled. It was a small, tremulous smile, but he took heart. He walked across the floor, running the gauntlet of what seemed to be a thousand eyes although there were less

than a dozen people in the bar and none of those knew
of his disgrace.

Suddenly, they were each uncertain what to do or
say. Silence hung heavy for a second. Amy broke it.
"Hello, you."

"Hi. Could you manage another drink?"

She gave a sigh of relief. It was going to be all right. "I
think they're serving dinner," she said. "I could manage
a glass of wine with the meal."

"Let's go through, then."

They settled at a table for two. A waitress brought the
menu and they ordered. Tony's appetite, usually healthy,
seemed to have ailed but Amy found that she was hungry
after the fresh air; and the menu was not, after all, haggis
and stovies but much what she would have expected in
one of the better hotels at home. The waitress returned
with their wine and then left them in peace.

"Well?" Amy said. "Did they smack your bottom?"

Tony managed a bitter laugh and then relaxed. "Not
quite," he said. "I think they left that privilege for you.
But damn near it. I've had a strip torn off me six inches
wide, an endorsement made in my log-book and I've had
to fill out forms for the Civil blasted Aviation bloody
Authority. There'd have been less fuss if I'd ravished the
chairman's wife."

"You couldn't," Amy pointed out. "She's bigger than
you are." She had some sympathy with the philosophy
that, if lax standards were allowed to creep in, some pilots
might soon be skirting even closer to disaster. But she only
said, "They're going to let you fly, then?"

He nodded. "It was touch and go for a bit. Whatever

I said, like having come all the way from the other end of the country, almost, and never being able to afford the trip again—"

"Liar!"

"—yes, but they didn't know that, they only said that it was irrelevant. I had to beat my breast a bit and don sackcloth and ashes and swear by all that they hold sacred – the Rule Book of the British Gliding Association, mostly – that I'd sinned before Heaven and in their sight, but that I'd learned my lesson and would never cut a corner again. Then they said that they'd let me fly but that they'd be watching me like hawks and if I even farted in the cockpit I'd be grounded immediately and probably for ever. They didn't put it quite like that."

"I'm glad," Amy said. "That they're letting you fly, I mean."

Tony met her eye. "Are you really? Even though it means I take the glider up tomorrow? That's generous of you."

"Yes. Does that mean," she asked carefully, "that if they'd grounded you, you were going to let me have your glider for the whole week?"

He shrugged. "Might as well have done."

It was easy, Amy supposed, to be generous in mere hypothesis. On the other hand, he was not being dog-in-the-manager and she could afford to be equally gracious. "Well I call that very handsome of you," she said. The tables were filling up, mostly with fellow competitors who were surreptitiously watching Tony. "And do you really want to fly tomorrow?" she asked. "You wouldn't rather swap days with me?" She waited anxiously. If he took her up on her offer, she rather than Tony might lose a day's flying to the weather.

"We'll leave it as it stands," Tony said. "They hinted that minds could be changed and that if I didn't fly I'd better be around helping with the chores or minds ruddy well would be changed. And I fancy hanging around on the airstrip, manhandling gliders and being stared at as if I was an incompetent idiot, even less than I fancy doing my thing in front of all those critical eyes."

"I don't know that I'd have the brass neck to stick around at all," Amy admitted. "You've got guts."

They talked, rather stiltedly, of other things for the rest of the meal.

At the close of the meal, the waitress put a saucer of flat, paper-wrapped after-dinner mints on the table. Amy had had a surfeit of sweetness but she took two. "I'll pocket these," she said. "I may get hungry on Tuesday."

Tony pursed his lips. "You're really sure that I won't wreck another glider tomorrow?"

"Don't be bitter," Amy said. "Of course you won't."

"Of course I won't." Tony refused coffee and went to his room.

He breakfasted alone and left early in the Range Rover.

Amy had slept restlessly, fretting more over her relationship with Tony than about her father's glider. She took her time leaving the hotel. At the airstrip, she joined the small gang of volunteers who were wheeling gliders and balancing each by supporting a wing at the moment that the launch began. Tony was waiting his turn. She had forgiven him, but seeing him in possession of an undamaged glider she felt a prickling of her dormant anger, not so much at his clumsiness as at his stubborn reluctance to utter any apology or admission that he had been seriously in the wrong. But, even so, she wanted him to do well.

Tony looked up from checking his instruments to find Amy beside him. For one joyous moment he thought that the constraint of the previous evening was gone and that she was still his dear friend. He prepared to utter the word of apology which would have been enough. But Amy's face was cold. "There'll be thermals under those clouds further up the valley," she said. "In this wind, you should be able to ride that far along the face of the ridge to the north. The south slopes catch the sun, so it's possible that you might gain some extra lift from anabatic wind. Don't waste your time looking for rising air nearer to here."

"Thank you," he said, "but I'll make my own mistakes."

The advice had been intended as an olive branch but at Tony's ungracious retort her indignation welled up again. "No doubt you will," she said. "And many of them." She went back to help wheel out the next competitor, leaving Tony to curse himself for his churlishness. Why was he always driven to say the wrong thing at the wrong moment? No wonder that he was eternally rejected by the one person who meant the world to him. He promised himself to mend his ways and guard his tongue.

One after another the competing gliders were collected by the tow-planes and took to the air. One of the earliest starters found a weak thermal over a farm and soon several gliders were circling in the feebly rising current of air; but

Tony, she noted with approval, headed for the hillsides. His pique had not blinded him to the value of her advice. There was hope for him yet.

When the competitors were all away, the launch point was more than adequately manned for the few non-competing club members who planned to fly. Amy headed for the clubhouse in search of coffee and a comfortable seat.

The big room was almost empty. Coffee was available even if comfortable seats were less evident. Amy fetched a polystyrene cup of coffee from the machine to a plastic-topped table and was about to lower herself into an uncomfortable-looking moulded chair when a voice said, "Amy Fergusson, surely?"

She turned. The nicely rounded young woman, of about her own age, in a pale summer frock of expensive simplicity, rang only a distant bell in her mind. The red hair, now professionally styled, provided one clue and the timbre of the voice another.

"Julia?" she said. "Julia Mason?"

They kissed the air several inches from each other's cheek, while recollecting several years of tepid friendship, a definite coldness during their last term together at school and an explosive, hissing and spitting row on the last day. Julia had overturned Tony's car and Tony had damaged her father's glider so that Amy, casting her usual logic to the winds, felt that Julia had somehow triggered a chain of disasters which had culminated in her presence today in the clubhouse instead of soaring with the rest and the seemingly immobile constraint between herself and Tony. Julia was recollecting, without pleasure, the embarrassment of trailing through the town to a final ceremony in the town hall on a windy day with no underwear.

They sat. Amy, in her working-and-flying denims, felt disadvantaged but she was damned if she would let the other see it. "You're looking very healthy," she said.

Julia's fixed smile faded slightly. She had always been sensitive about her tendency to plumpness. "You look just the same," she said. From what was either a very large handbag or a small holdall in alligator hide she took a stainless steel thermos flask and poured coffee into a stainless beaker, adding cream from a second, smaller flask. "I always carry my own," she said. "I do think that machine coffee is the dregs, don't you?"

Amy had not relished being compared to her earlier image as a gawky schoolgirl. She lifted her cup defiantly. "I'm told that machine coffee is really very good," she said. "But it always tastes exactly the same, which takes away any interest."

"I expect you're right." Julia moved her left hand so that a diamond sparked. "I'm here with my fiancé. Jasper Croll, you know?"

"Would that be Jasper Croll, the cook?" Amy asked.

Julia raised her eyebrows in disdain at this naiveté. "You mean chef. Actually, he's a restaurateur. Are you still going around with that boy – what was his name? – Tony Something?"

"Hope-Williams. Yes, I'm here with Tony."

Julia looked down at her own ring. "But you haven't managed to hook him yet?"

"I have never tried to hook him," Amy said, trying not to sound indignant. "We're just friends."

"I remember that you were both keen on these glider things. So's Jasper. He's up there somewhere now, trying to win something. Well, it keeps him off the streets. I seem to remember that you used to go gliding."

"I still do."

"But you don't have a glider-thing of your own?"

Amy decided to ignore the fact that the damaged glider belonged to her father. After all, what was his was as good as hers. "I did have," she said. "Tony bent it yesterday, so I'm flying his one tomorrow." Julia hid a yawn, imperfectly. Amy's nostrils flared. "Did you ever learn to drive?" she asked.

Julia's brow creased but she failed to think of a suitably cutting retort. "Excuse me," she said. "I must go to the little girls' room and put a new face on. Shan't be long. You might keep an eye on my bag."

She remained in the toilet for some minutes, keeping Amy waiting. This was a mistake. It gave Amy time to think and to prepare; and Amy was in no mood to be trifled with. When Julia returned, Amy, using considerable sleight-of-hand, contrived to slide an unwrapped chocolate mint onto the seat of her chair.

Nestling in what Amy thought might be an exceptionally cosy nook, the chocolate melted very satisfactorily. Amy lunched on sandwiches in her father's car and watched with sardonic pleasure as Julia strolled around, bestowing smiles and inconsequential chat on anyone who cared to accept her acquaintance. She remained unaware that the dark brown stain in the geometric

centre of her backside was responsible for at least some
of the smiles that she received in return until somebody
– some spoilsport, in Amy's opinion – took her aside
and whispered in her ear. She made a hasty departure,
but only to change her dress in her hotel for another,
equally flattering to the fuller figure. She was back at
the airstrip and darting poisoned glances at Amy before
the competitors started to trickle back and swoop over the
finishing line.

Some of the competitors came in exuberantly, sweeping
down from a height to cross the finishing line at high
speed and soar up into the heavens again, but Tony
landed without incident, making his approach by the
book and settling smoothly in the precise centre of the
runway as if to show the doubters that he could fly
well when he wanted to. He returned rather earlier in
the sequence than when he had departed. Amy was not
one of the group which assisted in rolling his glider back
to a place in the glider-park, but as soon as it was at
rest he beckoned to her. Amy resisted the impulse to
reply with a gesture of extreme vulgarity and walked to
join him.

Julia, appearing out of nowhere, got there first and when
Amy arrived was greeting Tony almost as if they were
former sweethearts being reunited after a long separation.
Tony, though flattered, soon assumed a hunted expression
and glanced at Amy, begging for rescue. But Amy,
confident that Tony felt no more drawn to Julia than
when they had last met and that Julia had no intention
of abandoning a mature and well-heeled fiancé already in
the bag for the uncertain prospect of the younger Tony,

assumed the expression of a mother observing her children at play and bided her time.

Tony was driven at last to break into the chain of how-are-yous and do-you-remembers. "Excuse me, but I must speak to Amy for a moment."

"Of course," Julia said. Her tone suggested surprise that he should waste his discourse on so unworthy a recipient.

Tony turned to Amy. His eyes demanded sympathy which was not forthcoming. "For tomorrow," he said after a pause, "there's only one battery – the spare was a dud and got taken out. Can we get it on charge?"

"The charging rack in the hangar's full," said one of the helpers.

"It shouldn't matter," Tony said. He took a voltmeter from one of the side-pockets and tested the battery. "It was fully charged before we left and today there was perfect visibility for navigation over the ground. I had the radio on for an hour in case there were any last-minute course changes, and that was almost all. It's still more than nine-tenths charged. There's plenty for tomorrow, but after that we'll have to put it on charge overnight."

"I'll see that you have priority," the man said.

"Thanks. Amy, I'll just run over the switches with you."

Amy was in no mood to be patronised by Tony. "I have flown this glider," she said. "Quite a lot."

"Not for more than a year – except for a few minutes yesterday. And I've just proved to everybody how the mind can go blank at a critical moment." Having effectively turned the tables on her, he devoted several minutes to a careful explanation of the electrical system. "All right?"

"I've got it," Amy said. She was damned if she was going to thank him.

"I must go and check in." Tony put his hand to the canopy.

"Leave the canopy up for the moment and let the smell of sweaty feet blow away," Amy said.

Tony flinched and turned away, hurt feelings in every line of his body. Julia linked her arm with his and as they walked away Amy thought that the other girl was whispering something about 'wrong time of the month'. Well, Amy thought, perhaps she had asked for it. Who was she to cavil at Tony's behaviour while she herself felt compelled to behave with an equal lack of grace? She must forgive and forget.

And there had been much in what he had said. She lingered for some time, familiarising herself again with the instrumentation and visualising the unfamiliar feel of the controls. Tomorrow would be a far cry from a simple flight around a target visible from the starting-point; and it would be too late to start groping for an instruction manual while in the throes of competition. Only when she was sure that the right reflexes would come to her aid, she closed the canopy.

When she reached the clubhouse again, the results of the day's competition were being posted.

Tony had been placed second.

Amy pushed through the chattering figures. Tony, feeling that he had redeemed himself, was holding his head up and looking around, defiantly. Julia still had him in tow but they had been joined by a lean, smiling man who Amy recognised from his television appearances as the chef and restaurateur Jasper Croll, Julia's fiancé.

Croll had a neat beard to make up for thinning hair. He was as neatly dressed as if about to give one of his cookery demonstrations on television, but he looked strangely unfamiliar to Amy without the customary apron. He shook Amy's hand warmly. "You're flying tomorrow, I believe," he said in the warm voice which sent a pleasurable shiver up a million female spines.

"God and the weather permitting," Amy said. She half-turned to offer Tony her congratulations.

Tony accepted them as his due. "Thanks," he said. "But – listen, Amy – this puts me in contention for the overall trophy. You're not still going to insist on taking over my glider tomorrow, are you?"

Any intention of forgiving, let alone forgetting, was forgotten. "Certainly I am," Amy said stoutly. She lowered her voice as the only alternative to yelling at Tony. "You're not going to have the nerve to suggest that I don't? I certainly did not come all this way and see you crash my glider in order to give up my flying on the off-chance that you might stay ahead of more experienced competition."

Julia could be counted on to take the side of any attractive male. "Oh, come on!" she said. "Give Tony a break."

Amy's voice began to rise despite her best efforts. "Like the break he gave me, breaking my bloody glider?"

Croll had more sense than to chide Tony directly but he addressed himself to Julia. "I think we should stay out of it," he said gently. "Miss Fergusson has every right to claim redress, in the circumstances." He put a faint but recognisable emphasis on his last three words. Evidently, detailed accounts of Tony's touchdown were still circulating. Croll returned his attention to Amy. "Am I right in thinking that your father is Colin Fergusson, the meteorologist? He's very good. I was organising a garden party at a stately home. We went ahead on his assurance that it would be dry until late afternoon; and he was right, almost to the minute."

For the first time in twenty-four hours, Amy felt a warm smile make an appearance. "I didn't realise that you were also Jasper Catering," she said. "My father's only just returned from abroad. I did that forecast for you. I'm glad it worked out."

"Amy held the fort for her old man for a year," Tony said, "and did it very well." Amy chalked up a mark in his favour.

Croll looked impressed. "Just between ourselves, what do you think are the prospects for tomorrow?"

Julia made an impatient sound and wandered out into the sunshine.

Amy had spoken to her father that morning. His advice would be available to anyone who did the same and paid his consultation fee, but Jasper Croll had taken her part in her argument with Tony. "Between ourselves?" she asked.

Croll said, "Absolutely," and Tony nodded.

"It's not difficult to see what's coming, but predicting *when* can be much more difficult. That forecast I gave you was in a much simpler and so a more predictable pattern

143

than we've got just now. There are several depressions heading this way," she said. "It's the aftermath of Hurricane Josiah. They're behaving unpredictably, but the signs are that they're speeding up. If they get even more of a move on, the leading edge could bring wind later tomorrow, probably from the west but veering."

"So an early start might be a good idea?" Croll suggested.

"That's what I'll be aiming for."

They were soon deep in discussion, Croll and Amy over tactics and Tony concerned whether there would be any competition at all on the Wednesday.

Out on the field, Julia wandered peevishly among the gliders. In her incomprehension, their slim elegance had no meaning for her. She had known them as rivals for Jasper Croll's affection and she had been right. He had even dared to correct her when she had stood up for Tony. Nobody wanted to talk about anything sensible.

She came to a halt beside a glider which she recognised as Tony's. The canopy was closed but she had seen how the catches were operated. She unlocked and raised it, reached in and switched on an instrument. She had no idea of its purpose but a needle flicked, so she assumed that current was leaving the battery. Glancing round guiltily, she closed and locked the canopy again. It was no more than an act of minor spite, soon to be forgotten. Her lack of understanding was so complete that she had a hazy vision of Amy missing her flight because of a self-starter failure and having to beg a jump-lead start from another pilot.

Seven

It takes more than one circumstance to create an incident. The first – Amy's annoyance with Tony – had already been in place. The second was Julia's malicious interference with the glider. The third was to follow shortly.

Amy did not see Tony again that evening. She received an invitation to dine with Jasper Croll and Julia at their hotel. Julia made little secret of her reluctance to have Amy added to her cosy *tête-à-tête* with her fiancé but, in the event, she had no cause to complain of being left out of what she expected to be an interminable conversation about gliders. Amy, now that her student days were behind her and her father was back at home, was counting on some leisure time, some of which she rather hoped to spend sailing on *Laughing Girl*.

"Crew really can't be expected to sit down with a knife and fork while racing in half a gale," she pointed out. "Food gets taken from the fingers or, preferably, out of a mug if at all. But how much real nourishment can one put into soup?"

"And not destroy it in the cooking?" said Jasper. "Interesting question . . ."

145

It was a question which dominated their conversation during most of the meal. Even Julia, who counted food as one of the few subjects of interest to her, joined in. They discussed ingredients which might retain both flavour and nutritional value in the cooking or which could be added immediately before serving.

"I'll do some research," Jasper said at last. "Go on watching my programmes. I'll do a special on the subject. And thank you for the idea."

By the time that Amy returned to her hotel Tony, convincing himself that Amy was deliberately avoiding him, had gone to bed.

Amy was at the airstrip early. She had every intention of being first in the air.

Tony, once the adrenaline rush of his successful flight had passed, had regained his sense of proportion. He was sure that the coldness between them had returned and, between bouts of feeling aggrieved and misunderstood, he knew deep down that his own selfish clumsiness was responsible. In the hope of making amends, he was determined that Amy should have every chance. He followed her car out to the airstrip and waited while she underwent the pre-flight briefing and collected the details of the day's competition. They walked out to the glider and carried out the Daily Inspection together. The sky was half clouded – referred to as 'four-eighths cloud' – and there was a light but rising breeze. Amy congratulated herself on her early start. Late starters might have a struggle to return on the upwind leg.

Amy's mood of optimism suffered a serious setback

when she raised the Perspex canopy and attempted to check the instrumentation. "Tony," she said, "your battery's flat."

"Can't be." Tony leaned into the cockpit and checked the connections to the battery terminals.

"It is." Amy stooped to look more carefully. "What's more, the variometer's been on all night. Look at it."

Tony looked. "That would be enough to flatten the battery," he agreed. "But you saw me, for God's sake. I demonstrated each instrument to you and switched it off as I went along. You *watched* me."

"I watched you but I wasn't *watching* you. Didn't you notice it when you closed and locked the canopy?"

"I didn't close the canopy. You did. Here! If somebody's interfering with the gliders we should tell someone."

"No time now," Amy said desperately. She wanted to scream and bite things but that would have accomplished nothing. Instead, she was trying to force her mind to work. "Tony, they haven't started launching competitors yet. Dash back to the hotel and fetch the battery out of my glider. Here's the key to the trailer."

"No good," Tony said. "I couldn't get at the battery without unloading the glider and I'd need help and . . . and . . ."

Amy accepted that her first idea was a non-starter. "I can still fly. I'll still have the airspeed indicator, the altimeter, the mechanical variometer and the magnetic compass. That's as much as anybody would have had a few years ago."

"But no radio. No electric vario, no turn-and-slip, no

horizon. Oh, and my GPS comes off the main battery."

"I can navigate without the help of a Global Positioning
Satellite, thank you. You didn't need to use it yesterday."

"The sky was clear. I could look down and know
exactly where I was. Tell you what – one of us could
pee in the battery," he suggested. "Well, I could. That
usually gives them a fresh lease of life."

"Don't be silly," Amy said.

Tony saw that Amy's face was set and her jaw was
thrust out. He was nagged by feelings of guilt. He was
also grateful to Amy, who could so easily have suggested
that he had flattened the battery in order to handicap her.
"Listen," he said. "Hang on for as long as you can. I'm
going to see what I can find. But in case you really have to
launch before I'm back, you'd better take this. At least you
can get messages and if you have to make a field landing
you can tell us where you are." He put his mobile phone
in a cockpit side-pocket. "Nought-three will get you the
race control here."

Amy was tempted to take issue with his assumption
that she might have to 'land out', but admitted to herself
that even the best glider pilots might occasionally run
out of height and have to set down wherever they could.
"Thanks," she said gruffly.

"It's OK. Good luck!" He set off at a quick jog towards
the hangar.

Two helpers had arrived to handle the glider. One of
them helped Amy with the straps of her parachute. They
laid hands on the glider.

"Not yet," Amy said.

It was a long way to the hangar. Tony arrived, breathless and sweating. The hangar was deserted. There were several batteries left in the rack but if he took one and the owner came for it, he would be as good, or bad, as a thief. He could leave a note. He looked for paper and a pencil. Hopeless!

There was one last option. A car battery would be heavier than the customary motorcycle battery used in gliders, but the extra kilos would only bring Amy's light weight up to that of a medium-sized man. The terminals should fit. Whether there would be space for it . . . But problems were for solving. The cars were behind the clubhouse in quite the wrong direction. He started running again.

Time, which drags its feet while the impatient are fretting, can gallop away just when it is most needed. The forecast had promised wind. Word had gone round and competitors were hurrying into the air. The breeze was rising. Amy had lost her advantage. If she waited longer she might lose her chance as well. She stood up but she could see no sign of Tony. The queue of gliders had vanished. The tow-plane was taxiing into position and the Launch Point Controller was beckoning. Amy settled into the cockpit, closed and locked the canopy and fastened her straps. She jotted down the course for the first leg, added the magnetic variation, made an allowance for windage and set the grid compass accordingly.

The launch routine went quickly. Amy found herself airborne before she had time for a mental review of her plans. Looking down, she saw the Range Rover scurrying over the grass like a beetle.

Tony, looking up, saw his glider already airborne and he drew the Range Rover to a halt well clear of the runway. Almost immediately, he lost sight of the glider in cloud.

Amy 'pulled the bung' at 2,000 feet and looked around. Smoke from a stubble-burning suggested a strong thermal and she swung towards it. She had time to glance earthward again and then at the compass. Something seemed to be slightly out of gear, but she was arriving at the thermal and needed all her concentration to search for and hold the best lift. The smell of the smoke was unpleasant and she closed the ventilation, but at least the foul air was carrying her upward. The climb took her through cloud. When she emerged, there was no other glider in sight, just the apparently endless undulations of innocent-looking clouds. Another, much higher, layer of cloud obscured the sun, so at least heat and dazzle were not going to be problems. She brought the compass card into line with the grid and set off, watching for her next thermal. To the joy of flying was added the zest of competition. She was enjoying herself.

Amy's father plotted the last data from the Met Office on the overlay to his map, added the figures thrown up by his computer program and stared at the result. It was only too clear what had happened. The high sitting over the south of England had added its weight to the depressions which were rotating in the contrary direction to the north of Scotland, accelerating them along their track and adding wind to wind. The radio which he kept turned down to a mutter in the corner of his office-study was only now beginning to warn of imminent gales. He grabbed for the phone. There were a dozen clients who should be warned. But one call came at the top of the list. The number was engaged. He put the number on redial and sat back. He found that he was sweating.

The Club Secretary was in the small office, monopolising the phone while he argued with one of the club's regular suppliers over a wrong order, which had, in any case, been delivered late. When at last, with a sigh of exasperation, he hung up, the phone rang again immediately. He sighed again and lifted it, prepared to be terse with the caller. Phone-calls to club secretaries are seldom good news.

"This is Colin Fergusson," said a voice. "Is my daughter there?"

The Club Secretary was able to open the door without leaving his chair, thanks to the compactness of the office. He looked out. "I don't see Miss Fergusson," he said. "I think she's already launched."

"I advise you to recall everyone and scrub competition, at least for the day. The weather system has been moving faster than predicted. It's freak weather. There could be some dangerously strong winds, generally from the west."

The Club Secretary thought swiftly. He knew Colin Fergusson's name; the club had used his services on occasions and his predictions had been almost uncannily detailed and accurate. Also, his voice had been stressed. "Leave it with me," he said quickly. "And pass me any more forecasts as soon as you can make them. On fee, of course."

He hurried out of the office. Outside, a non-competing glider was being hooked to the tow-plane. He ran forward, raising his arm to the vertical and shouting, "Stop!"

The glider had been a hundred yards away but even in the rising wind his voice carried. All activity halted. The Launch Point Controller, the wing holder and the forward signaller each raised an arm to echo the signal. The glider pilot released the cable. The Secretary gave the plane's pilot the switch-off signal and doubled back to the clubhouse.

The Competition Secretary was at a table in the big clubroom, sorting entry forms and totting up the entry fees. "What the hell's going on?" he asked plaintively.

"Message from Colin Fergusson," the Club Secretary said rapidly. "Freak weather on the way. Very strong winds from the west. Better cancel for the day. How many are already up?"

"All of them."

"Get them back. They should be upwind of here, thank God!"

The Competition Secretary sifted through the entry forms. "They all have radios but they may not be listening."

"Tell anyone who acknowledges the message to signal to anyone who doesn't seem to have got it and then get down quickly and carefully."

"Is it really that bad?"

"When Colin Fergusson gets panicky it's time for others to do the same. Look outside."

Outside, in the rising wind, one glider had been blown over. Scurrying figures were making safe any gliders not already tied down or weighted on the upwind wing with old tyres. The Competition Secretary turned to the radio. The Club Secretary went out to make sure that everybody knew that competition was off for the day.

High above the lower clouds, Amy did not know that she was being swept to the east. Her attention was absorbed in flying the machine while at the same time carrying out complex calculations in dead reckoning with a view to descending through the clouds with the turning-point already in sight. The temperature had dropped and the cloud cover had closed below her, but the whole air-mass was progressing eastward and she seemed to be gliding through relatively still air. Even the brief judder as the front overtook her had not been out of the norm. She had no way of knowing that she had entered controlled airspace, but between her airspeed and the movement of the air mass she was through it and away before she could endanger anybody. The air traffic controllers put the faint blip on the radars down to a flock of birds.

She looked at her watch. By dead reckoning, she should be nearing the first turning-point. She began a descent, very slowly because she would be over hills.

As she passed over Aberdeen, the city's thermal swept her upward in the cloud. Her eyes were wide open for the first sight of the hills so that she missed the sudden movement of the variometer. When next she glanced at the altimeter she was shocked to realise that she was back again at over 5,000 feet.

*　　　*　　　*

"I raised most of them on the radio," the Competition Secretary said, "including the three who aren't competing. They have each other in sight and they can make it back here. We'd better have parties out beside the runway to grab them as they land and before they blow away again. But nobody's seen any sign of Miss Fergusson and I can't get her on the radio."

Tony had come back to the clubhouse to get what news he could and he overheard. His face blanched. "She doesn't have radio," he said. "There was a battery problem. We suspected tampering. I gave her my mobile phone as a substitute." The Competition Secretary took the name of his Lord in vain, coupling it with certain biological expressions not usually heard in polite company, and apologised quickly to the nearest lady. "Why in the name of Moses didn't you give her one of the Club's hand-held radios?"

Two spots of colour appeared on Tony's white face. "Didn't think of it. Didn't know you'd lend them. Didn't have time to ask. I was fetching another battery but she took off anyway."

The Competition Secretary looked at him down his formidable nose. "It's not been your week for being clever, has it, my son? Phone her, then. Tell her to get back here if she can. If she can't, she's to pick somewhere flat and sheltered and get down before it gets worse. Competition's off."

Very red about the ears, Tony picked up the phone.

Amy came out of dark cloud to see below her a grey expanse of sea, striated with wind-driven waves and

flecked with white. For a few seconds she was disori-
ented, unable to comprehend the impossibility of it. Had
Scotland sunk beneath the waves? Such changes took
whole millennia, they did not happen suddenly, in less
than an hour. She circled once, fighting down panic. This
was an occasion when only methodical thinking could
stand between herself and getting her feet wet with almost
certainly fatal results, but where could thought begin when
there was no valid starting point? She could see a coast
and, far beyond, a line of hills, but she had nothing like
the height she would need to return, against and across
what was obviously a strong wind.

The cause of this disaster was irrelevant and the time
available to her in flight would no doubt turn out to be a
critical factor, but she could not resist another glance at the
erring compass. It told her that the land was to the north of
her, which, unless she had strayed off course for a matter
of several hundred miles, was the one direction in which
land simply could not lie. She needed help. Somebody
else might be able to make sense of it or to position her
by cross-bearings. Tony had put his mobile phone in the
side-pocket. She snatched it out. The compass turned and
settled. Land was now to the west of her, which made
sense. The land to the west was Scotland, which had
been inevitable all along, and, to judge from the seaway,
the wind seemed to have backed towards the south. She
cursed Tony for stowing the phone so near to the compass
and – she looked at it – for leaving it switched on. But,
of course, she realised suddenly, she was not being fair
to Tony. He had not been the unthinking designer who
had positioned the compass so close to the side-pocket,

and the phone would have had to be on if she were to receive messages. She clicked it off angrily – the compass twitched a few more degrees – and dropped it into one of her pockets.

Only seconds later, Tony received a recorded message to tell him that his phone was not in use.

Amy looked around desperately. Land in the distance, beyond reach. There were several oil rigs towards the other horizon, two of them showing the bright orange spark of a gas flare. They might be too far away to reach, but with the wind behind her she might come near enough to be seen and rescued. Perhaps if she used Tony's phone to send a message through the coastguards, the oil rigs could be alerted to watch for her.

She put a hand to her pocket, but in the same moment she saw a chance of salvation, a miracle to rank with the *deus ex machina* of a classical play. A tanker was heading south, butting into the seas and throwing up sheets of spray. It looked small from her elevation but it represented safety in the face of disaster. She considered using her parachute, but God alone knew where the wind would take her. If she flew past the tanker's superstructure and then ditched the glider ahead of the vessel, they would surely see her and pick her up. She would have to ditch gently to stay afloat. Carbon fibre, she thought, was not buoyant.

A ship, she seemed to recall, needed a long braking-distance. Somebody had mentioned a mile, but in the context of what size of ship she had no idea. She would have to ditch well ahead.

She put the nose down and swooped. The tanker grew

until it looked enormous. The glider was being bounced in the turbulence of the air. The airspeed indicator was over the "Maximum Rough Air Speed" displayed on the Limitations Placard but, between the real wind and the ship's speed, she was overtaking the tanker only slowly. Its flat deck reminded her of an aircraft carrier and out of her chaos of thoughts it struck her that she might as well crash on board as into the sea. That way, she could save her camera and many of the glider's instruments and components and also save herself from a cold and hazardous ducking. The airspace between the superstructure and the stubby foremast was clear. Her mouth was dry and there were cramps in the lower part of her body.

She came up on the tanker from behind and to port, careful to allow room for the long wing and to keep both wings well clear of the wave-crests. She was suddenly aware that she could hear her heart pounding. The problems in geometry and physics which were being posed were no part of the glider pilot's curriculum but her background in meteorology had given her an intuitive understanding of air currents. She positioned herself and applied the air-brakes only to find that she was losing the height and speed necessary to get past the superstructure. Just beyond her starboard wing-tip a large radar antenna was rotating and in a moment of whimsy a corner of her mind thought that the screen would probably light up and say 'Tilt!'. She returned the airbrake lever and the glider eased forward again. But she was running out of height. It was now or never, time to act and hope, time to put her faith in God, in her own skill, in Tony's forgiveness and in

157

the intelligence of the designer who had produced a superb flying machine and then sited the magnetic compass near the side-pocket. It was time to fly by the seat of her pants and hope that she could keep them clean.

No lookout was being kept to the aft of the tanker. What would overtake them in that seaway? The helmsman was taken by surprise and swore loudly in a strong Belfast accent as the shape went past the windows of the bridge. His first, mad thought was that a pterodactyl left over from the age of the dinosaurs was attacking the ship, looking for an easy meal. The port lookout ducked instinctively.

Instinctive caution made her keep the long wings clear of trouble. Amy eased the glider across the wind, to get above the deck. The glider took a buffet from the air being pushed ahead of the superstructure and she thought for a heart-stopping moment that she had hit the guard-rail with a wing-tip. The deck was not as uncluttered as she had first thought. There were hatches and ventilators and all sorts of unidentifiable protrusions put there especially to embarrass visiting gliders. There was no time to think it out, only time to react. Her best chance was a single, large, central hatch. It offered a flat surface to touch down on. Whatever befell after that would be in the lap of the gods. All that she wanted was to survive.

She arrived over the hatch, bouncing in the turbulence. This was going to be a bad landing. Well, serve Tony right, it was *her* turn to bounce *his* glider. She again applied half air-brakes, lowered the nose-wheel and found that she was holding station a few feet clear of the hatch. Two men had been doing something with ropes near the hatch and she saw their faces turn very white in the poor light. She hesitated, for fear of slicing into them with a wing, but the decision was taken for her. The tanker rose to a seventh wave, the hatch came up under the glider. Cushioned by the rising air, the two met as gently as if she had been setting down on tarmac on a calm day. Instinctively she eased the control column forward microscopically and applied full air-brakes and wheel-brake.

She expected the two men to leap around in panic, shouting stupid questions and shaking their fists at her, but with wondrous presence of mind they darted in and each caught and steadied a wing-tip. She shouted to them not to put weight on the wings, but as much of her voice as escaped from the canopy blew away on the wind. And the warning proved unnecessary. Seamen become used to handling all kinds of loads. They held the glider safely.

Amy expected a sudden calm. Instead, she felt increased motion. The tanker was moving more violently than the glider had done.

Tony put down the telephone. "I gave her my mobile phone ready switched on," he said. "But the recorded voice keeps telling me that there's no response."

"Keep trying," said the Competition Secretary. "You get places where reception's terrible."

"Not up there."

"But is she still up? She must have set down somewhere that there's no signal strength."

"God, I hope so. I just hope that she hasn't blown out to sea."

"In this wind," said the Competition Secretary, "she's

probably in bloody Norway by now. Should we alert the coastguards?"

"What could we tell them?" the Club Secretary asked. "We can't give them a location. We can't even be sure that she isn't walking around, looking for a working phone so that she can tell us where she is. We'll hear soon enough if she's been seen crossing the coast."

Amy's hands were shaking. She had to fumble with her straps and then with the locks of the canopy. It was a struggle to raise and hold the canopy while she climbed out into the noise of the wind, leaving her parachute on the seat and locking down the canopy behind her. One of the men beckoned to her and she walked unsteadily to join him. Her knees felt loose and she was almost unbalanced by the unfamiliar movement. She felt the chill of the wind begin to bite. She was dressed for the greenhouse effect of the cockpit and her clothes were soon damp with spray. She started to shiver but the well-being of the glider was more important than mere comfort. The tanker heaved to a sudden swell and she felt heavy and then, for a moment, almost weightless.

"Well done!" she said. "Oh, well done!" Amy had to speak up to make herself heard over the whine of the wind and the hissing of the sea. Between the large hatch and the superstructure she saw that there were two smaller hatches side by side. "Could we move her there, with the fuselage between the two hatches?" she asked.

The man caught on immediately. He nodded, put two fingers to his mouth, whistled and waved an arm. Two more men materialised, apparently out of nowhere. They seemed well accustomed to working together. One or two words and a hand signal were enough. Amy took the tail and with one man at each wing-root and one at each tip the glider was gently moved backwards. It settled comfortably, supported by its wings on the two hatches. The air being pushed in front of the superstructure was comparatively still and there was less tendency for the glider to take to the air again.

"We need weights and cushions," she said. "Old tyres?"

"Leave it to me," he said. "That's my sort of job. I'm bosun and first mate and just about everything else. You just hold her." He stripped off his oilskin jacket and put it onto Amy. She was lost in its folds but it kept her dry and some warmth returned. The man, in his woollen sweater, seemed perfectly comfortable.

Amy and one man were left to hold the glider. The ship was moving to the rhythm of the seas and the deck was slick so that sometimes it seemed to her that she was hanging on to the glider rather than holding it down. Her hair was becoming plastered in rats' tails down her face.

The bosun seemed to be gone for a long time but he returned with several old tyres, a lot of rope and some battens, and the men soon had the glider securely but gently supported by tyres under each wing, roped and weighted. So far as Amy could tell, there was no damage apart from a few superficial scratches in the glossy surface.

"Now Miss," the Bosun said, "you'd better come with me."

"One moment," Amy said. She was eager to get into warmth and shelter but suddenly realised that the mobile phone might not work inside so much metal. She took it out of her pocket. "I'd better let people know that I'm safe."

"Not just yet," said the bosun. He took the phone firmly out of her hand and dropped it into his own pocket. "The skipper wouldn't like it." He led her through a door into the superstructure, closing it after them and shutting most of the noise outside.

"Now, just a minute!" Amy exclaimed. Her voice came out much too loud and rang between the metal walls. She repeated herself in a normal tone.

"Just a minute is right," the bosun said. He had an accent which Amy first thought was American, then Australian, but finally pinned down as Belfast.

"But they'll be worried sick about me."

"Their relief will be all the sweeter when they hear that you're safe. I expect you could do with a mug of tea?"

Tea, warming and nourishing, was just what Amy wanted most in the world, even before assuring everybody of her continued survival. She followed him meekly along an alleyway and into a windowless space, furnished with tables and chairs, which was evidently some sort of crew-room. The metal walls had been painted an institutional cream some years before. The door closed behind her, but when she looked round she was alone. There was the sound of a bolt or lock.

Amy had no capacity left for surprise. Being safe was enough and having Tony's glider safe was a bonus beyond price. She sat down and laid her head forward on her arms on one of the tables, exhausted by effort and fear and ready to sleep anywhere. But the Bosun was back almost immediately. She heard the door click and open and he came in with two mugs of tea held by the handles in one hand and deftly balanced against the ship's movement. He sat down opposite her. She now had time to notice that he was short and rather rotund. His head was as round as a bowling ball, but with a snub nose and tiny ears. His black hair was thinning and what remained had been cropped close to his head. But on that unpropitious beginning had grown a friendly and even modestly good-looking face.

"Well, now," he said. "You pose a bit of a problem."

"I must do," Amy said grimly, "if you have to pinch my phone and lock me in. What the hell's going on? I got blown out to sea. I had to make an emergency landing. If you put me ashore on solid ground anywhere that suits you, I'll be properly grateful for ever. So what's the problem?" She tasted the tea. It was sweet and rather too hot for comfort but otherwise it was good tea. She began to come out of her dazed state but she was still thinking through a layer of treacle.

The man shrugged. He rolled a cigarette neatly between his fingers and licked the edge of the paper. He raised his eyebrows momentarily at Amy before lighting it, which he seemed to consider a token request for her permission. "Can't do any harm to tell you," he said at last. "This old tub's been sold to a Norwegian syndicate. She delivered her last load near Belfast and the crew were paid off. We're a scratch delivery crew. We're due to deliver her in Oslo some time tomorrow – empty and with clean tanks. So we drained the tanks and flushed them out. We did it coming through the Pentland Firth during the night. It was cheapest that way."

The renewed supply of body-sugar was enabling Amy to work up the rage which she felt was due. "And just what has this to do with me?" she demanded. "And by what right did you take my phone away?"

. The Bosun refused to be rattled. "Aren't I just telling you?" he asked calmly. He took Tony's mobile phone out of his pocket, removed the battery and handed the phone to Amy. The battery he dropped into his pocket. "You'll get this back when we bid you a sailor's farewell. Listen now. You'd have figured it out in the end anyway. We must have left an oil slick thirty miles long in the Pentland Firth and the environmentalists will be hopping mad when they hear about it, so no way is the skipper going to tell the world we're at this place at this time. He'd be in all sorts of trouble, hauled up, fined more money than he'll see in his lifetime and maybe his ticket or his seniority taken away from him."

"Uh-oh," said Amy.

"Now you're beginning to understand. I went up to the bridge first thing after you dropped in on us and he told me to put the glider over the side, one piece at a time. I've talked him out of it . . . for the moment."

"He wouldn't really do that would he?" Amy exclaimed, aghast.

The Bosun laughed without any pretence at mirth. "You don't know him. He's a Catholic from Dundalk and they come kind of ruthless. My guess is that he's maybe waiting a while rather than leave the bits floating where he wouldn't want anybody to know he'd been. The question is whether he'll want to throw you after it, but if I get the first officer on my side we can maybe persuade him that once we've docked and flown home it'll be no more than your word against ours. We picked you out of the water wherever we wanted to pick you out of the water. Is there any proof of where you came down?"

"Not that I can think of," Amy said. She had already admitted the urgent need to phone. She had become almost proof against seasickness on *Laughing Girl*, but the motion of this monster was very different. In the confined but moving space, smelling of diesel oil tainted by the smell of his cigarette, she was beginning to feel sick. Her mind was beginning to work again but she did not like what it was telling her.

"There you are, then. We've just turned to cross to Norway but the skipper's keeping a log which shows us passing north of Shetland and cutting through the gap between the oil and gas fields. If you try to tell a different story we'll tell ours, how you were doped to the eyebrows, too stoned to know where the hell you were."

"But—"

"No buts," he said sternly. "Can't you see that I'm on your side? Go along with it all the way or you'll be up against a man who spends his shore time drinking with members of an IRA splinter group. I could put it stronger than that but I won't, because I don't go in for frightening girls – unlike some of them. And the crew is in his pocket."

"Including you?" Amy asked.

"Including me."

The Bosun's manner remained friendly but Amy was in no doubt that she was between a rock and a hard place. It would serve Tony right for bending her father's glider and being an arrogant sod who looked down on her just because her hormones were female. And at the same time she knew that she was being unfair, that Tony was only the way he was because he was insecure, which was partly her fault for putting him down, and she wasn't going to let his glider, his pride and joy, get broken up and dropped in the deep, not without a fight.

"I want to speak to this captain of yours," she said.

The Bosun's eyebrows slid up. She might have been asking for an interview with the devil. "It won't do any good. It may even do harm."

"I don't care. I want to see him. That glider isn't even mine. It belongs to a friend and his father's one of the richest men in Britain. He's probably a member of the syndicate that bought the ship."

"I damn sure wouldn't tell the captain that," said the Bosun. He wagged a finger in a remarkably old-maidish gesture. "In the skipper's view, rich Englishmen come somewhere between child molesters and Oliver Cromwell. He's a busy man and a careful one, but if you want a word with him I'll see what I can do. Can't say fairer than that, can I?"

Amy thought of claiming that she and Tony and Mr Hope-Williams were all Catholics and hailed from some-where in Ulster, but she knew that she could never have posed successfully as Irish in her present company. "No," she said, "I don't suppose you can."

She was left alone again, locked in with the cigarette smoke, the smell of oil and the slow lift and plunge of the ship. She was feeling distinctly unwell. Her scalp prickled and her stomach seemed to have been borrowed from an intemperate stranger. Part of her malaise was the result of being too hot and she realised that she was still wearing the oilskin jacket. She shrugged it off and dropped it on a neighbouring table.

She wondered whether the time might not have come when tears or a tantrum would be the proper response but decided that logical thought was still her only course. Her mind was feverish but she pushed her malaise out of her mind, as far as it would go, and while she combed her drying hair out with her fingers she reviewed her options.

She had demanded to see the captain without a thought in her head except that she simply had to influence him, plead, threaten, somehow tamper with fate. But what to say? This would have to be good or the glider would go over the side, quite possibly with herself in it. Silently she rehearsed a succession of speeches but decided that none of them would have satisfied herself in the captain's place.

The wait stretched on as though time had become a loop. She stretched out along the seats of half a dozen chairs and closed her eyes. To her surprise and relief, her stomach settled. And one desperate, forlorn argument crept into her mind. *When all else fails tell the truth*, she decided. If she came safely home, she thought, she would have the words carved up or tattooed somewhere private.

She was beginning to doze when the door clunked and opened and the Bosun came in. "Skipper's busy," he said. "I've brought the first officer."

Amy sat up, pulled her skirt down and tried again to restore some sort of order to her hair.

The man behind the Bosun was tall and lean with a saturnine face and black, spiky hair. He towered over her, looking down on what she felt must be a scarecrow figure. Amy's instinct was to get up but she felt that by remaining seated she was somehow demanding the privileges of weakness and femininity. Just at the moment, she needed every privilege she could get. Her previous experience of the Irish had been of warm and friendly people, so kindly that they would tell you what they thought you wanted to hear rather than the truth. Despite his words, the Bosun had seemed come from that stock. Confronted by the first officer, Amy saw how the same root could also produce a very different breed of men.

"What did you want to say to the skipper? You can say it to me." His voice had the flat, metallic twang of Belfast.

Amy forced herself to speak slowly and not to babble. She managed to put the faint suggestion of a brogue into her voice. "That glider belongs to a long-standing friend of mine," she began. "Tony, his name is."

The First Officer frowned. "Where do you come from?"

"My mother was a Malone from Hollywood, County Down." It was the truth except that she had omitted two generations. For a moment she expected him to ask whether she was Catholic or Protestant and she was in an immediate dilemma. She had had several Catholics among her school-friends and she might have been able to sustain that particular pretence, but if the Captain was Catholic did it follow that all of his crew were the same?

But the First Officer seemed to be unconcerned with sectarian matters. "This Tony. Your sweetheart?"

"No, he is a bumptious, arrogant bastard. We came up to Scotland for a major competition." Remembering her Irish great-grandmother, a redoubtable old lady who had lived to receive her telegram from the Queen, Amy struggled to keep a trace of a brogue in her voice, but as soon as she diverted her mind to practicalities her English accent took over. "On Sunday, he wrecked my father's glider and last night he tried to get out of giving me a turn in his glider – this one – for today's competition, on the grounds that he might be in line for a trophy but I'm only a girl and wouldn't get half a mile up the road. And I'm a better glider pilot than he is, that's exactly what gets up his nose."

She paused for a moment. She was being hard on the absent Tony, but he would never know. And she sensed that the attitude of the two men was softening. "Today, he handed the glider over with a flat battery so that half the instruments didn't work, including the radio, and to take the place of the radio he gave me his mobile phone switched on and put it in the cockpit near the magnetic compass, and that's what threw me off course. I'm so furious that I could spit—" Amy paused again and swallowed "—and it would serve him right if you did dump his glider in the sea."

The First Officer looked unimpressed. "So what are you saying?"

Amy found that her arguments had laid themselves out in front of her. She found that she was beginning to grin in spite of herself and her discomforts. "Nobody's ever crossed the North Sea by glider. It's possible in theory but it's never been done. You get no thermals over water. If

I'm the first to do it, he'll go mad with rage and jealousy. He'll explode into a trillion tiny bubbles of envy and there won't be a damn thing he can do about it. I'll be very modest and sympathetic and that'll just rub salt into the wound.

"What I'm saying is that if you're going to be off Norway just before first light and if you can find some way of launching me so that I can make it to land, do you think I'm ever going to tell anybody that you gave me a lift across? I want the credit for being the first. I want to set a record which will stand for years and I want to rub his nose in it."

There was a dead silence apart from a dull throb of the ship's engines and a hissing of the seas against the hull. Amy's stomach fell and she closed her eyes. It had been a mad idea and she had failed.

Then another sound made itself heard. Her eyes snapped open. The First Officer had begun to chuckle. His face, from being saturnine, had creased into what, for him, must have passed for jollity. His sudden shout of laughter bounced around the metal surfaces of the room. "Heaven save us all from a woman who's looking for revenge!"

The Bosun was grinning. The First Officer looked at him. "Well, Spike," he said. "I'd sooner oblige the lady if we can. I'd rather she had a good reason to hold her tongue than that we had to prove her a liar. Is it possible to do what she wants? Could we launch her?"

Both men's faces lost their smiles and became thoughtful. Amy realised with amazement and relief that they were taking her mad idea seriously.

"You should have picked yourself an aircraft carrier,"

the Bosun said thoughtfully. "They'd've had no problem. What speed would you need?"

"About fifty knots. That's airspeed, of course," she said quickly when the Bosun's face fell. "Knock off the ship's speed through the water."

"We don't have a winch that would give quarter of that speed," said the First Officer.

"There's ways," said the Bosun. "You know what an eight-part tackle is?" he asked Amy.

Amy's sailing experience came in useful. "Two blocks of four pulleys each," she said promptly. "It gives an eight-to-one increase in force."

"And you know what I mean by the fall?"

Amy lost patience. "Would you know what I meant by a male chauvinist pig?" she demanded.

The Bosun drew himself up. "Of course – we have every sort of pig there is in Ireland, I'll have you know."

"Well, you're as bad as Tony is, still treating me like a silly little girl. For Christ's sake, I have a physics degree and I was crewing on *Laughing Girl* when she came second in the Fastnet race."

"Well, I wasn't to know that," the Bosun said, crestfallen.

"You know now. The fall is the emerging rope that you pull on."

The Bosun nodded, but he said, "Not necessarily. If you have that physics degree and you've been crewing on the ocean racers, you'll know what happens to the fall if you pull the two sheaves of an eight-part tackle apart?"

She began to see what he was getting at. "The fall's

drawn in eight times as quickly. But it's no good launching me at sea level with barely flying speed."

"With an arrangement of tackles, I can give you any speed you want."

Amy felt a surge of hope but at the same time her mind was racing ahead, searching for snags. "That's in theory," she said. "In practice, I'm not sure you could give a glider enough acceleration over the length of your deck without tearing it apart. And you've all those obstructions. You'd have to give me a clear runway for at least half the length of the deck."

"How wide?"

"At a guess, two metres should do it."

The Bosun shook his head slowly. "I've not got a quarter of the timber for that."

"So it's impossible," said the First Officer. His face hardened.

"Wait a minute," Amy said hastily. "There's one other way. Is this wind going to hold?"

"I've listened to every forecast in the last few hours," said the First Officer. "They don't all agree, but the consensus is that it'll back a few degrees but it won't drop much until late tomorrow. It may even strengthen. What's this other way?"

"It's called kiting. You fly me literally like a kite. Add the wind and the ship's speed together and I should have enough airspeed. You give me a pull with the winch to get me started. Once I've taken off, you can pay the rope out slowly. I can climb on the end of it whenever you give me another pull. When I have all the height I can get, I release my end of it. Do you have rope aboard?"

The Bosun seemed relieved to be brought back into practical discussion. "Rope?" he said. "Miles of it! I don't know what that other lot were up to – unless they thought they were on the *Cutty Sark*. And it's polypropylene, most of it, so it floats. No danger of getting it round the screws when you drop it off."

The First Officer thought for a few seconds, his eyes half closed. "I can sell it to the skipper," he said. "But how do we know you're on the level? You could be ashore before we made land and have the authorities waiting for us."

"We've only to say she was that lost she didn't know whereabouts in the North Sea she was," the Bosun pointed out. "Anyway, she couldn't think up such a tale, tired as she was, without there was truth at the back of it."

"I'll buy both those arguments," the First Officer said. "I think the skipper will go along. But it'd better work. If you end up in the water, you're on your own and we've never even heard of you."

Eight

In the darkness before dawn there was no let-up in the wind. From time to time, moonlight filtered through the hurrying clouds. Otherwise, they were dependent on torch-light to supplement the light of a single lamp on the superstructure and a glow spilling down from the bridge where the captain, an aloof, bearded figure, was pretending to be unaware of the goings-on below.

Amy had managed a few hours of sleep in a borrowed cabin and had been given a meal, surprisingly well cooked. The remainder of the time had been spent evolving a launching drill with Spike, the Bosun. Then, while the seamen had been bringing seemingly enormous amounts of rope up from some distant store, he had helped her to carry out the Daily Inspection although for once no entry was made in the Daily Inspection Book. Spike had even offered to charge the glider's battery; but this, she suspected, was a test of her forethought, because he had only nodded when she pointed out that a charged battery would contradict the story which she would have to tell.

A few sparks of light and the faint glow of a distant lighthouse were all that revealed the presence of the coast. Now, suddenly, she was aware of seeing the outlines of the hills against a faint lightening of the sky. The glider had been moved forward to the large hatch where it had first touched down and four seamen were steadying it by the wings. Other dim figures were standing by, to observe the unusual launching or in the hope of witnessing calamity. As they approached land, the ship's motion had become more violent.

Spike had found a shackle to fit the cable release, and the end of the rope mountain, leading away to the forward winch, had been spliced on. She got rid of her borrowed oilskin jacket and felt the cold begin to eat into her. She settled herself into the cockpit, still holding the canopy by its edge with both hands. "Remember," she said. "I'll need a good pull to get me clear."

"About sixty metres. I'll remember."

"Then when I get up into stronger and steadier wind—"

"I begin to pay out."

"And you give me another pull on the winch at intervals—"

"Just the way we've been discussing for the last hour and more."

It was clear from his voice that Spike was losing patience but, in her state of nerves at attempting a winch takeoff from a moving deck in the dark, Amy found that silence was beyond her capability. "When the weight of rope gets too much, I'll release. Otherwise—"

"Otherwise, if I'm running out of rope, I'll give you a flash with the signal lamp," he said patiently. "I'll remember."

"And when I get up and clear I'll be in stronger and steadier winds—"

"And I can pay out a bit quicker. I've got it. Now for the love of God, get going or we'll be in full daylight and you won't see my lamp but you'll be seen from the shore."

"Sorry. I'm a bit overwrought." Amy licked her dry lips. "That's it, then. Thanks Spike. God bless!"

"And good luck to you too," he retorted.

She closed and fastened the canopy, shutting out the chill of the wind and most of its noise, fastened her straps by touch alone and ran quickly through the control checks again. Spike's figure faded into the gloom. Moments later the slack was taken up on the cable.

She waited, going over the agreed drill in her mind. The wind was coming over the starboard bow, so she would get to port to escape the rebound of the wind from the tanker's structure. Spike, at the winch, was waiting for the perfect combination of sea and wind. She hoped that his judgement would be sound. Perhaps she should have borrowed a lamp to signal him when—

It came, a heavy gust as the tanker rose to a head sea. There was a short blaze of light from Spike's signal lamp. The seamen stepped clear and Amy balanced the glider on its main wheel before immediately easing back the control column. The pull of the winch came softly – the rope had more stretch than wire cable.

Before she knew it, she was airborne and being tossed in a black void. She felt more stretch of the rope cable. There was just enough light in the dawn to give her a horizon to help her keep the wings level and the glider's attitude nose-up, but she had to think clearly and use all her senses to overcome the handicap of not being able to see instruments or controls or even her own hands. She waited with gritted teeth to be slammed back to the deck or against the ship's railings, or for the stretch in the rope to allow the glider's tail to foul the tanker's superstructure; but the flow of air became steadier and then a few faint lights against the dark sea resolved themselves into the ship ahead of her and below and she realised that Spike was already paying out the tow. She sucked, trying to make a little spit to swallow.

Vision seemed to arrive suddenly as the daylight grew. There was enough light now for her to make out the ASI and she adjusted the angle of attack to obtain the optimum airspeed. She could feel the changes in pull as Spike followed their plan of action. The weight increased as more and more rope was fed out, but she was still gaining height when there was a bright flash of light from below. She pulled back on the control column to make as much height as she could and then fumbled for the cable release lever, pulled it firmly. After a heart-stopping delay the cable fell free and she felt the glider jerk up. She levelled out and turned. She had enough height to reach the coast, she kept telling herself. She wagged the wings once in farewell.

Daylight was still growing. Soon she could see a low cliff and rising ground beyond. She was riding in what seemed to be calm air but with a substantial drift in the wind. The hillside was rough, too rough for a safe landing, and the wind would be blowing across its face, offering no helpful lift. Having come so far, it would be cruel if she crashed at the last moment.

A little further downwind, there was a deep bay and a promontory beyond. She adjusted her course, turning downwind. With the speed of the wind, there was little time for conscious thought. There could, there should, there *must* be lift up the face of the hill beyond. She arrived over the surf with little height to spare but the variometer at last showed a rate of climb and the altimeter began to wind upward. She turned inland, to make the most of the hill lift. She was climbing, climbing in the turbulent air above the ridge, but all too soon she was carried over into 'sink' and began to lose what she had gained. The ground was still too rough for a safe landing, all hummocks and boulders and never a clear strip between. The variometer gave another kick and she turned into wind again. She climbed a hundred feet in a few seconds and then lost touch with the lift. She could be ahead of it or behind, she had no way of knowing and no time to experiment. She held downwind, to cover the maximum distance while she looked for a landing area.

Time became blurred. There was no spare mental capacity to record its passing. There was only a blur of constantly struggling to maintain height and to watch for a safe landing area. Later, when she consulted a map, she was amazed to see how far inland she had flown.

At last, without warning, there was salvation ahead. She came over another crest and there was a field of grass sheltered by a row of pines.

In the lee of the hill, the wind might be doing almost anything. She swept over the trees, allowed a little extra margin and made her turn. She saw a barn and a small farmhouse and cattle sheltering beneath trees but the grass was clear. She left the air-brakes until the last moment. The air was very turbulent but she managed a passable touchdown and coasted in to halt by the barn.

The glider was stable, starboard wing down in a cowpat. She sat still for a minute, yawned hugely and let the adrenaline rush begin to subside, but she could not relax for more than a few seconds. The cattle, curious as cattle everywhere, trotted across to investigate this unfamiliar arrival. Cattle, she knew, were one of the worst hazards to a parked glider, licking or chewing the surfaces or standing on the wing-tips. She dragged her straps free and threw up the canopy. The cattle, which had never before been cursed in the English language, retreated a few yards and formed a semi-circle, becoming a fascinated audience.

There was a human voice behind her and she turned. A man, the farmer she presumed, was standing beside her. He was a stocky figure in dungarees. He had a round face, wire-framed spectacles and a cap pulled down hard over his head against the wind.

Cautiously, Amy raised the canopy the rest of the way but in the lee of the barn it was at no risk. She completed her climb out into the chill wind and closed the canopy behind her. "Do you speak English?" she asked. She found that she was enjoying the surprising immobility of the land.

"Little." He paused, gathering up his vocabulary, pointed to the glider and then to the barn. "Better in there."

"Yes." Amy looked at the cattle and then at the barn. "Safer from cows," she agreed. There was no way that the glider would go inside with the wings rigged. She sighed. The favours she had to do for Tony . . . She brightened as two large young men came out of the house. "My sons," the farmer said proudly.

"How do you do?" Amy said politely. She began to strip the tape from the nearest wing-root joint. She was becoming desperate for a pee, but she could wait a little longer.

Several hours later, the glider was safely de-rigged and in the barn and Amy, warmed and comforted by a huge mug of thick soup, was using Tony's phone to speak to her father.

"Thank God!" Mr Fergusson cried. "We've all been worried sick. Tony's hardly been off the phone."

"Is that right?" Amy said.

"Yes. He wants to know where his glider is."

Amy's lip curled of its own accord. "If he calls again, tell him that it's in a barn near Egersund. That's in Norway, tell him, in case he doesn't know. Listen, Dad. The farmer's going into Stavanger and he's going to give me a lift. By good luck – probably the devil looking after his own – I have a credit card in my purse, but I've never had a passport, so I'll have to find the consulate or something. I'll try to catch a plane some time tomorrow. I'll phone again. Tell them they can stop looking for me. Got to go now. Cheerio."

Acutely conscious of the cost of international calls by mobile phone, she disconnected. As she did so, her father was saying something else, something about a book, but it had no meaning for her preoccupied mind. Anyway, it could not have been important. She would remember to ask him when she saw him again.

*   *   *

Stavanger turned out to be a town consisting mostly of brightly painted timber buildings. The journey, in a little DAF which had seen very much better days, seemed to take for ever and the consulate, by the time they found it, was closed.

The farmer dropped Amy off at a small hotel. They parted with half understood expressions of mutual esteem and promises to look after the glider and (on Amy's part) to keep in touch. She slept for eleven hours, ate a hearty continental breakfast and was on the doorstep when the consulate opened in the morning. There she ran up against the buffers of bureaucracy and was shunted from one office to others. It seemed that it was the day of the visit of some foreign Royal and all but the most junior and least experienced diplomatic staff were attending. She could not be repatriated as a Distressed British Seaman because she was not a seaman, nor, she pointed out angrily, was she distressed by anything other than the run-around she was receiving. She could not be given a replacement passport because she had never had one in the first place. And she was without her birth certificate. She could, it seemed, be anybody from an Iraqi spy to an aspiring immigrant eager to take employment away from British workers. If her birth certificate were sent out to her . . .

Amy found herself on the doorstep with her mind in a whirl. She would have to phone her father again. She had no intention of lingering in Norway, waiting on the uncertain postal system. Remembering the amazing sum still lingering in her savings account, she could probably afford a courier service. How did one contact such a body?

Her father would probably know – he seemed to know everything else. And, in the meantime, she would have to get passport photographs, renew her reservation at the hotel and buy some toiletries and a change of clothes.

She was still standing there, trying to sort her options into a rational sequence, when a rather stout woman in a hairy coat leaped ponderously from what Amy took to be a taxi, put away a mobile phone in a fat briefcase and came panting up. She was sweating slightly and, Amy noticed, she had a faint moustache. "It is Amy Fergusson, isn't it?"

There was no discernible accent but Amy was in no doubt that the woman belonged in London. She did not seem to have any official status, but who could tell these days? Even to be returned to England in handcuffs would be preferable to being stranded indefinitely on foreign soil. She admitted her identity. "Do I know you?" she asked.

"Not yet, but you will. Thank God we've caught up with you at last," the woman said. "I'm Hilda Jenkinson. Far-out TV Productions. I've been trying to get you on your mobile number."

"The battery ran out and I didn't have a charger." Amy frowned. "How did you get my number? It isn't even in my name."

"Your publisher gave us your home number and we spoke to your father. We want you to appear on the Harold Davidson show tonight. Fee . . . twelve hundred. All right?"

"I suppose so. But there's a snag. I don't have a passport."

"So we discovered. We got your birth certificate and a

snapshot from your father and he signed the form for you and I've brought you a BVP. British Visitor's Passport," she added when Amy looked blank. She produced a document bearing a photograph which Amy recognised, with a pang, as having been copied from a photo of herself and Tony. "And we've booked you a room in the Palace Garden Hotel for tonight after the show. All right?"

The prospect of being interviewed on television terrified Amy, but at least she would be back on home soil. "All right," she said. "If I have time to get my hair done."

"Makeup can do that for you." Ms Jenkinson produced a clipboard. "Sign here," she said briskly.

In the taxi to the airport, Hilda (as she insisted on being called) extracted from Amy and wrote on her clipboard the precise address of the farm where the glider had landed. As she emerged at the airport, she waved to a small and tired-looking man who collected the page from her, handed over an envelope of tickets and, without a word being exchanged, took over the taxi. He was carrying, Amy noticed, what seemed to be the original of the passport photograph. "I'll want that photograph back," she told Hilda.

"Of course, dear."

She never saw it again.

The tickets were evidently for a superior class of travel. Amy, an inexperienced traveller, was only vaguely aware of the difference, but they were admitted to a quiet lounge, away from the hurly-burly of the common herd, to await their flight. Hilda was solicitous in providing coffee.

Amy could have occupied the waiting period in admitting that the glider had made most of the crossing as deck cargo on a tanker and to express surprise that anyone might have thought that she had flown all the way; but the news that Tony had been concerned only with the well-being of his prized possession had hardened her resolve. If she could, she would go through with it; she had spent the intervening waking hours polishing her story.

Amy had seen the Harold Davidson Show although it was not her favourite viewing. It occupied a peak midweek slot and so was presumably popular, but Mr Davidson – Hal, as he insisted on being called by the better-known among his guests – was sycophantic to the good and great but his manner to lesser mortals was often overbearing or hostile or even downright bullying.

"What does Mr Davidson want to ask me about my trip?" she asked.

"Just a few technical details. And of course about the book."

The book! Amy's mind had been fully occupied with gliding and associated problems for the past forty-eight hours. The book she had dismissed from her mind as probably having no impact and being soon forgotten. But now she was going to have to answer questions about it. A once familiar sensation returned to her from her student days, of going into an examination while realising that she was inadequately prepared.

"I've been out of circulation for the last two or three days," she said. "I missed the publication day party. What's been going on?"

Hilda Jenkinson threw up her hands. "Going on? My dear, what hasn't? It's the literary sensation of the year. Tremendous reviews and already there's talk about a film. You'll make a fortune. Other companies will be after you, but you've signed with us, remember."

Amy's mouth returned to its familiar dry state. "It's quite a long time since I saw the proofs," she said carefully, "and much longer since I wrote it. I ought to refresh my memory. Where can I get hold of a copy?"

Hilda dug into her briefcase. "I have one here. When the idea of the show was mooted, the office begged several copies from your publisher and I pinched one to read on the plane. And I must say that it brought back some beautiful memories. Would you sign it for me? If they ever ask for it back I'll buy them another copy."

"Yes, of course," Amy said dully.

She had never even seen a completed copy. The author's copies would have gone to Derek Cardinal's house and presumably he would share them with her. She received from Hilda a substantial volume. The dust-jacket was embellished with the title *A Feeling of Love* – which had been agreed, Derek Cardinal had told her, after endless argument – and had been executed in delicately harmonious colours. The artist had depicted two eyes, one obviously female and the other male. The outlines of the brows and cheeks were no more than faint silhouettes. The space between formed the shape . . . but no, that surely was a thoughtless coincidence. The background was faintly floral.

So far so good.

Amy began to read and continued on the plane to

Bergen, during the short stopover and the longer flight to London. She omitted the sections which she had read in the typescript and skipped lightly over several lengthy digressions.

Her first impression, that it was a beautifully written love story, was confirmed, but she found that, by ill luck, her earlier sampling of the typescript had missed some explicit accounts of sexual activity. These were in only the mildest sense pornographic, although some of the activities were rather more enterprising than what she had been led to believe was the norm. The incidents were not described with salacious gusto and there was no direct attempt to arouse the reader. The encounters were described with the same gentle sensitivity as the rest of the story and with as much poetic imagery; but the reader, herself, had an immediate sense of being present between the sheets, a favoured observer, and Amy felt a flush of embarrassment creeping over her. As she read on, she became a participant rather than an observer. Derek Cardinal's research must have been remarkably thorough and his sources outspoken, because she was able for the first time to confirm that the strange sensations which she had become aware of while exchanging caresses with Tony were the symptoms of arousal . . .

If she had given the typescript a proper reading when she was given the chance, would she still have agreed to lending her name, she wondered? In a way, she had been lucky. She had been spared the need to agonise over the question. Now all that she had to do was to agonise over *another* decision. She could take the credit, hide her blushes and spend the money wisely. Or else she would have to break her promise to Derek Cardinal and, presumably, give the money back.

She began to fret. Tony would think that she was writing from experience

Hilda Jenkinson dropped her, by taxi again, at the hotel. Amy was shown to her room by a supercilious porter and she was discomfited to realise that she had almost no cash with her for a tip. Her first action, even before going out to the shops and a cash machine, was to phone Derek Cardinal. She wanted to be released from her promise of secrecy. But there was no answer from his number.

In desperation, she phoned her father. "I'm back in London," she said. "I'm staying here tonight and I'll be home tomorrow. I'm being interviewed on the Harold Davidson Show this evening. Please don't watch it, but you could tape it for me if you insist. Where can I get hold of Mr Cardinal?"

Her father's voice dropped half an octave. "Haven't you heard? No, I suppose you wouldn't. It only happened on Monday evening."

"*What* happened?"

"I hate to be the one to tell you this. I know that the two of you were becoming close. He told me more than once how much he enjoyed your company. I'm afraid that he had a gliding accident. He crashed into the side of a house."

"He can't have done," Amy said dully. "He was usually thought of as the best pilot in the club."

"My dear, skill doesn't save us from the ravages of age. When they got him to hospital, they found that he'd had a stroke, a bad one by all accounts, followed by serious injuries in the crash. It seems to be touch and go. He's in the London Clinic."

"Could I get in to see him?"

"You could try, I suppose. But from what I've heard, he might not recognise you."

"Thanks, Dad. I'll see you tomorrow."

"*Don't hang up.* Please, tell me what's going on." Her father's voice was plaintive. "How did you get to Norway? What are you being interviewed about? Is it your flight or this book that's getting all the publicity? Did you really write it? Why couldn't you tell me about it?"

"Tomorrow," she said. She hung up. "Perhaps," she added.

Amy had time for a quick bath, a panic visit to the shops and a square meal before the car was due to return with Hilda Jenkinson to take her to the studios. She seemed to be getting by on one proper meal a day, so weight gain was not going to be a problem.

At the shops, she chose a dress of jersey silk and of carefully calculated length, because she had decided to give the viewers a look at her legs (to distract them from the possible inadequacy of her answers) but would prefer that her knickers were not also on view. Just in case of a miscalculation, she treated herself to some rather special underwear on the supposition that even if nobody else saw them they might bring her confidence.

The car arrived to collect her, rather later than she had expected. Whisked away to the studios, she was taken in hand by a make-up girl who tutted at Amy's outdoor skin, and by a hairdresser who sighed over her curls, phoned somebody to find out which of Amy's profiles would be to the camera and then styled and fixed her hair in a manner which looked good on television and simply awful in the street.

Hilda had developed a fixation for the clocks which were distributed liberally around the walls and yet she seemed to Amy to be dawdling. From the idle talk on chat shows, Amy had been led to expect a preliminary meeting with Harold Davidson and a drink in Hospitality, but instead she was kept hanging around in one untidy office after another and led through devious passages, with the result that they arrived in the studio only seconds before the broadcast was due to begin. The studio was smaller than it had been made to look on the few occasions when Amy had watched parts of the show and, outside of the area occupied by Mr Davidson and his guests, scruffier. A studio audience was crammed into seats rescued from some demolished theatre.

Harold Davidson was gifted with rather obvious good looks, of which he was noticeably conscious. His hair was carefully waved and he was dressed for television in a dark suit by a top tailor and a pale blue shirt which would not dazzle the camera, with a tie which could have betokened a guards regiment, a gentleman's club or a public school but not one which Amy, who had received instruction in such important matters at Bath Ladies' College, recognised. His handshake was limp and cursory and he seemed glad to get rid of her hand as quickly as possible by pointing her to one of a group of three chairs. Amy remembered suddenly that he had recently 'come out of the closet', announcing his homosexuality with a pride that amounted almost to a fanfare of trumpets. This had been greeted with applause by the gay community and those who considered themselves to be liberal.

There was another man in the third chair, a thin man but with a pot belly. His bald head had been carefully powdered. There seemed to be no time for an introduction. "Don't move around more than you have to," the host said. "Smile whenever you feel like it and just give us factual answers to questions. You can manage that?"

"Yes, of course," Amy said. She said a few words while sound levels were checked and then braced herself.

Suddenly, they were on the air. A disembodied voice announced the show over a short burst of theme-music and Harold Davidson began his introductions. "Tonight, we have Amy Fergusson, the noted author of a novel which has received a great deal of publicity in the few days since it came out. But, even more remarkably, she claims to have flown a glider during the same period from Scotland to Norway, a feat never previously accomplished.

"To discuss this with her, we have Graham Dunn from the British Gliding Association. Over to you, Graham."

All became clear to Amy. She was to be sacrificed for a public spectacle. An inquisition was being sprung on her. Perversely, this made up her mind for her. She had still been half inclined to make a clean breast of her deception but she now decided that – damn them all – if she was to go down, she would go down fighting. She arranged her face into the appearance of openness and honesty which had sometimes deceived her teachers at school.

Graham Dunn looked at her coldly. Neither Amy nor

the viewers could be in any doubt that he disbelieved her story. "Miss Fergusson," he said, "you're recorded as having taken off from Aberdeenshire on Tuesday morning, taking part in a gliding competition. By dawn the next day you and your glider were in Norway. That was the same glider?"

"Certainly," Amy said. She remembered the man who had taken over the taxi at Stavanger airport. "I've no doubt that that the identity of the glider has already been checked. If it's of any help to anybody, I took photographs to confirm my arrival, but I haven't had a chance to get them developed yet."

Mr Dunn's mouth tightened. "In fairness," he said, "it must be said that unexpectedly strong westerly winds prevailed throughout the period. Even so, and accepting that you were flying a modern competition glider with a very flat gliding angle of about one in forty, such a flight would only be possible starting from a height of around fifty thousand feet or ten miles – close, in fact, to the world altitude record."

Amy felt happier. Mr Dunn had not done his homework. Perhaps he too had been whisked in front of the cameras without adequate time to prepare. She had managed to figure out the telltale lights on the cameras and she was aware that the live camera was staring her in the face. She was careful to keep her face composed. "At least let's start from a correct arithmetical basis," she said reasonably. "It doesn't need Einstein to work out that, from ten miles up, a glide angle of one in forty would give you four hundred miles. To that you'd have to add the substantial contribution of a stiff tail-wind. The distance between my starting point and where I landed is three hundred miles, give or take very little. Land miles, that is."

The lights on the cameras blinked. Focus had shifted to Mr Dunn's face, catching for a moment an expression of surprise and dudgeon. He made a quick recovery. "You seem to have given some thought to the matter. You were quite correct in assuming that the glider has been visited. Your altimeter shows that you had never been above seven thousand feet or about a mile and a half. That would be sixty miles at a one in forty glide angle. Even if you double that figure for the tail wind, that's only a hundred and twenty miles. It's unfortunate that none of your electronic instruments were functioning. Unfortunate – or incompetent."

Amy forced a smile. "Now, there I agree with you," she said. "It is unfortunate. I was not flying my own glider, which had been damaged – by somebody else. I was promised that the battery was fully charged. As it turned out, the electronics were left switched on all night – and I may say that I intend to get to the bottom of what may have been a malicious act."

"Surely it was folly to take off at all."

There was no point denying what might be seen as the obvious. Amy chose her words carefully. "Perhaps. It could certainly look that way in hindsight. But an easy course had been set for the day's competition. When I took off, the cloud cover was patchy – no more than about four-eighths – and the strong winds were not expected for some time, probably not that day. I had all the mechanical instruments – the variometer, altimeter, airspeed indicator and magnetic compass – pretty much all that any glider pilot would have had not so many years ago. Because I was without radio, somebody lent me a mobile phone and put it in the side-pocket. Unfortunately, meaning no harm, he put it there switched on. As I expect you know, on that model of glider the starboard side-pocket and the magnetic compass are not far apart and I discovered, later, that the phone produced a serious deviation in the compass. So, without knowing it, I was heading out to sea instead of up Deeside. At the same time, the cloud cover closed below me and the strong westerlies arrived ahead of time. When I came down below the clouds, I was already over the sea. In the wind that was then blowing, I had no chance of getting back to the coast. I had to go on."

Graham Dunn frowned and glanced down at a small page of notes which was hidden from the cameras behind his crossed knees. "Accepting for the moment that you could have been the victim of a whole series of unfortunate coincidences," he said, "and without bandying any more arithmetic with you, starting from seven thousand feet it would still have been quite impossible for you to fly to Norway in a straight glide."

Harold Davidson broke in. "Stay with us," he said. "We'll return to the subject after the break." He leaned back and blew out a breath. "Relax, folks. The porkies are going out."

"Why did you cut me off before I could answer?" Amy asked him angrily.

The other man smiled, showing pink gums. "I didn't ask a question," he said. "Nothing to answer."

Time was too precious to be wasted in off-camera debate. Amy held her temper in check and thought hard, choosing from the possible lines of argument in her mind one which Spike, the Bosun, had suggested to her. If she had had any thought of confessing, the smug and patronising disbelief of the two men had blown it to the winds.

"Now," Davidson said suddenly, catching her unprepared, "when we left for the commercial break, Mr Dunn had just said that the flight that Miss Fergusson claims to have made was impossible. And he is a very experienced glider pilot and a senior member of the British Gliding Association."

"All the same," said Amy, "he is mistaken. He's been making assumptions. He's assumed, for instance, that the help from the tail-wind would only have equalled the performance of the glider. And—"

"Miss Fergusson," Davidson broke in with exaggerated patience, "why don't you admit that this was a publicity stunt to bolster the sales of your book?"

"Because it was not," Amy snapped. "It happened exactly as I have said, unintentionally. And the coincidence of dates was nothing to do with me. I didn't choose the dates for the soaring championships nor for the publication of my book. Are you suggesting that I whistled up the westerly winds which only arrived when I was already airborne?"

Davidson looked into the live camera and shrugged elegantly. "I'm not suggesting anything except that the flight you claim to have made never took place. How else do you explain having claimed a flight which Mr Dunn tells us is manifestly impossible? Let us into the secret of the trick and we'll say no more about it."

"There was no trick," Amy said. "The flight took place."

"It couldn't," Dunn said abruptly. "There are no thermals over the sea."

"Ah!" said Amy. It was the chance for which she had been waiting. "Now see where you've made your mistake." She waited, smiling a smile which she hoped would look natural after the cameras had done their worst with it.

"I *beg* your pardon," Dunn snapped. "It's a well-known fact."

"I think that you should check your well-known facts before relying on them. What you've said is generally true but some seas are exceptional. The North Sea is one of them. It's dotted with oil rigs and every now and again one of them will burn off unwanted gas. I flew from rig to rig, looking for flares and whenever I found one I got a kick upwards to about seven thousand feet, quite enough to let me glide another sixty miles even without the tail wind. Each time, it carried me at least as far as the next flare and I knew that even if I ran out of height and had to ditch in the sea I could have done it close to a rig with a good chance of being picked up."

Graham Dunn looked down at his notes without finding anything to help him. "I don't believe it," he said.

"What don't you believe?" Amy asked gently. "That there are oil rigs? That they flare off gas? That—"

"I simply do not, can not, believe that a gas flare could produce a useable thermal."

Amy shrugged. She might just be getting away with it. "You can believe whatever you want to believe," she said.

Some signal must have passed. Harold Davidson, in close-up, chipped in, sensing it as the ideal moment to call a halt while Amy was still at a disadvantage. When the director switched back to a longer-range shot, it was seen that Mr Dunn and his chair had both vanished. "We shall soon be running out of time," Davidson said. "We've reached the point at which the studio audience is usually invited to ask questions of the guest. Would anybody . . . ?"

A large man rose. He was thick-set, expensively dressed but in need of a haircut. An assistant materialised beside him with a microphone. "It's not a question," he said. "I want to tell you something. I'm what they call a directional driller. I make frequent trips out to oil and gas rigs. Once, when the helicopter I was in was approaching a rig, they started to flare off gas. They're not supposed to when there's a chopper in the vicinity, but it can happen. Well, when hot air goes up, cold air has to rush in behind – Mr Dunn should know that as well as anybody. We dropped like a stone and were swept in towards the legs of the rig. Our pilot turned away and put on all power but I didn't think he was going to make it and when he pulled free at last, believe me, I thought it was Christmas, I was so glad to be alive. Having felt the power of a gas flare, I reckon the young lady has the right of it. A glider could get a hell of a kick upstairs."

There was a murmur from the audience, even a patter of applause, and a rustle as each individual relaxed.

Harold Davidson was in a quandary. The little bitch had not only slid out of the trap, she had gained the support of the audience. Instead of continuing with questions, he decided to switch to the alternative topic for discussion. "In the remaining few minutes," he said, "I'd like to ask you about your book. It does seem to go into detail – some might say unnecessary detail – about the sex act. Were you writing from personal experience?"

"No comment," Amy said, smiling, she hoped, enigmatically.

"The writing conveys an impression that the reader is in the room if not actually in the bed."

Amy was ready for that line of argument. "That is the objective of good writing. Authors may write about space travel, reincarnation, murder or blackmail or even death without having experienced any of those things. It's necessary to do some research and to use some imagination."

"And you have not, then, ever been raped by a gang of Hell's Angels?"

Amy's first thought was to reply, 'No, that'll be next Thursday,' but while she was still seeking a better answer she heard her voice saying the one thing which was, in the context of Harold Davidson's known orientation, unforgivable. It was later to be condemned all round on the grounds of political correctness, but the clip seemed to surface with remarkable frequency on shows made up of such excerpts. In some opinions, it led eventually to Harold Davidson's disappearance from the broadcasting scene. It was said in all innocence and the implications only dawned on her when she heard the audience react.

"No," she said. "I never fancied that. Well, I mean, would you?"

Nine

The broadcast was brought to a conclusion, which seemed to Amy unusually hurried. Before she was ready for it, the theme music was playing and a voice-over was inviting the viewer to tune in next week when the guests would be three famous celebrities of whom Amy had never heard. Harold Davidson hurried out of the studio, giving the impression of a man already late for a prior engagement with God.

The audience reaction to Amy's retort had been strong but, although one or two shocked cries were heard, not generally unfavourable. There had not been the conventional applause but rather an appreciative murmur and the muffled undercurrent of laughter produced by a considerable number of people, all simultaneously trying to stifle their amusement. As the audience filed out, there was a steadily rising babble of comment.

Amy, ashamed that her impulsive tongue had uttered what she now recognised as an apt but cruel jibe, hurried out through the nearest door. There was no courtesy car waiting to whisk her back to her hotel. Nobody at the studios even shook her hand or thanked her for her participation. As she found her own way out through the labyrinth of corridors, word had gone around or the programme had been widely relayed, because she had the impression of a drawing-aside of skirts and a few secret smiles. Her fee, however, did eventually arrive through the post.

She was wide awake and London was still bustling. She decided that there was one essential visit to be made. A taxi took her to the London Clinic but it seemed that she would not be allowed in to see Derek Cardinal. Positively no visitors were permitted. A reward for unremitting persistence was an interview with the night sister in charge of the Intensive Care Unit, a strong-minded lady who crackled with starch and crumpled dreams.

"You're not a close relative?"

"I'm a close friend," Amy said. "And I have a special reason for wanting to see him."

The sister, who had seen it all before, looked Amy up and down, taking in her dress, her rather theatrical makeup and her asymmetrical hair-style which, viewed full-face, was undeniably weird. In the sister's experience, there was only one possible connection between a distinguished old gentleman and a young tart. "Mr Cardinal is not well enough for visitors," she said, "and he's made it clear that he doesn't want any of his *close friends* to see him as he is now."

Amy felt herself flush. "I wouldn't upset him. I really wouldn't."

The sister nodded. Amy would not get the chance to upset him. "He would be very unlikely to recognise you," she said.

"In that case, I'd go away quietly and there would be no harm done."

The sister lifted her chin. "He is not allowed visitors. I can't put it more plainly."

Amy was tired, and especially tired of being interviewed in a hushed corridor. "If he's awake, will you please tell him that Amy's here? Then, if it's what he wants, I'll go away and stop bugging you. And the same if you tell me truthfully that he's asleep."

The sister's attitude, her voice, even her posture changed. "Are you Amy? Amy who?"

"Fergusson."

"So you're the Amy the patient's been asking for. I thought . . . I expected somebody older."

"Don't judge me by the way I look just now," Amy said, and she added, "I've just been on television."

The sister was unimpressed. She was quite used to nursing people far more important than television personalities. Politicians. Heads of State. People with *proper* jobs. But she unbent a little further. "Come with me," she said. "We'll see if he's awake."

Derek Cardinal was in an obviously high-tech bed, heavily bandaged and attached to a drip and to monitors which echoed, in sound and vision, almost every one of his bodily functions. Given half that amount of electronics, Amy thought, she would never have been carried out over the sea in Tony's glider. Cardinal himself looked small and very old but his face at least was undamaged. His parted lips revealed a full set of teeth, so Amy presumed that these were his own.

A nurse, sitting at the bedside, was dividing her attention between the patient and a nursing textbook. She looked up. "He's asleep just now," she said softly, "but he wakes up every few minutes."

Amy retreated out of the cubicle doorway and beckoned to the sister. "How bad is it?" she asked.

The sister met her eye for a moment and then looked away. "See me before you leave. The office at the end of the passage."

So the news was bad. Amy's spirits slumped.

The nurse appeared in the doorway. "He's waking up now," she whispered.

Cardinal's eyes were open. He groaned and stirred. The movements in the room caught his attention and he lowered his eyes from the ceiling. The left-hand half of his face smiled while the right remained fixed and glum. "Amy," he said from the side of his mouth. His voice was faint but there was no doubting that he was pleased.

"I came as soon as I heard," she said. "I've been abroad."

He turned his head slightly and looked at the nurse and her superior. "Leave us," he said. "Please."

The sister eyed the monitors. Evidently they showed nothing untoward. "You can go for your break now," she told the nurse. To Amy she said, "I'll know from the monitors if anything's needed, but you can call me if you get worried."

"Thank you," Amy said huskily.

"Come and sit beside me," Cardinal told Amy. She perched on the chair where the nurse had sat. It was a singularly uncomfortable chair, intended, she supposed, to guard against the night-nurse falling asleep. He moved his left hand slowly towards her. She took it and felt his cold, dry clasp. "How's the book doing?" he asked her. His voice was becoming fainter and she had to lean forward to make out the words.

"Very well, I believe," Amy said. "I honestly haven't had time to find out."

"Yes. The championships. How did you get on?"

Amy was beginning to see the funny side of her adventure and she was tempted to make a long and humorous story out of it, but she did not want to tire him and, on reflection, the fewer people who knew the truth the better. "Tony got a second," she said.

"But you?"

"I think I've set a new distance record."

He seemed satisfied. His mind was still on the book. "You've kept our secret?"

"With difficulty," Amy said. "Does it still really matter to you?"

His grip on her hand tightened for a moment. "Yes. I told you why. You know, I was surprised when you agreed to be my *alter ego*. I thought that the subject matter might be rather strong meat for you and put you off."

Amy was not prepared to admit that she had never read most of the book until that day. "But it's beautifully written," she said. "You must have had some fun doing the research." He managed a faint smile. "I never gave you a cheque for your share of the second advance," Amy said.

"It's not going to matter now. Keep it."

She hoped that her tears would not show in the dimmed light. "It will be waiting for you."

He squeezed her hand gently and rolled his head from side to side. He seemed to doze off. She was about to slip out when he opened his eyes suddenly. "Perhaps I shouldn't tell you this," he said. "But it was your book all along."

"Mine?"

"Yes. I based the girl, Shona, on you."

She was half amused and half appalled. Shona, once past her first hesitations, had taken to sex with all the enthusiasm of a child in a sweet-shop. But above any other emotion, she was flattered. "Do you really think that I'm as promiscuous as that?" she asked.

"I don't mean in that way. When the book opens, that's you. There you were, so innocent and so desirable. I found myself thinking of the joys and the agonies that were still to come to you. The dangers you would face. The ecstasy you would give some lucky fellow."

She had to probe further. "And the man, Bernard. Is that Tony?"

"Only at the beginning." He smiled his lopsided smile again and for a moment she could see him as he had been. "Later in the book I found that I was thinking of myself as I was forty years ago."

"You were a bit of a devil."

"I was, wasn't I? You haven't been embarrassed about the content?"

Amy accepted the return to a less emotive subject. "A little. I've just been on the Harold Davidson show."

"I meant to warn you to avoid that one. He's vicious. He gave you a going-over?"

"He tried," Amy admitted. "But he asked me whether, like the incident in the book, I'd ever been raped by a gang of Hell's Angels."

"You could give him an honest answer to that."

"I could. But, before I had time to think about it I'd asked him whether he'd have fancied it himself. He didn't take it too well."

Cardinal began to laugh. The breath rattled in his throat and he started to choke. Amy grabbed for the bell-push. The sister came running. "Wait in my office," she said.

It was twenty minutes before the sister joined her, by which time Amy had found a toilet and washed away the tears and, with them, most of the television make-up. The sister brought two cups of tea. "He's on oxygen and one of the doctors is with him now," she said. "He's come through it this time but, in all honesty, the outlook's not good. Between the stroke and the injuries, he couldn't take the surgery that he needs and on top of that . . ."

"He's old," Amy said for her.

"Yes. But when he came out of it he seemed cheerier. You must have done him good."

"I made him laugh. That's what started it off."

The sister put down her teacup and looked at Amy sternly. "Don't you go thinking that you've done any damage. I always think that it's important to give them something to enjoy. Frankly, I'll be surprised if he makes it through the night. But if he goes, he'll go happier."

"May I see him again before I go?"

"Better not. He's asleep and he'll sleep for several hours. Phone in the morning and if he wakes up at all you can come and see him and don't be afraid to make him laugh. I'll leave word with the day sister. But don't be surprised if it's bad news."

"Thank you," Amy whispered. Under the starched apron there dwelt, apparently, a heart of gold.

Amy arrived late back at her hotel, immensely saddened. Derek Cardinal had been one of the people who were always around, fixed points in a shifting world. Despite the disparity of their ages he had become a dear friend. His vanishing would leave a gap in her life.

"No messages," said the receptionist. "But there was a Mr Hope-Williams asking for you. Mr Hope-Williams Junior, he said. I think he's in the residents' lounge. Shall I have him paged? Or will you join him?"

Amy was in no mood for celebrating. "Tell him that I'll be in my room, please," she said.

The receptionist wore the uniform of receptionists everywhere although her hair was styled for the contemporary disco culture, but she was old enough to remember when stricter rules had prevailed. She raised her eyebrows at this flouting of convention but agreed.

In her room, Amy washed off the remains of her make-up and tried to restore some sort of normality to her hair. She was still struggling with the latter when there came a rap on the door. She refused to be hurried but shortly opened the door to admit Tony. A smell of whisky came with him although he was quite sober. His mood of depression was a perfect match for hers. He hugged her briefly. "Oh Amy!" he said. "I am glad to see you."

"Are you really?" she asked. "You don't sound very glad. Or are you more concerned about your glider?"

"Bugger the glider! I've been worried sick."

"Dad told me that when you phoned him it was the glider you asked for news of."

Tony took a seat on the bed. Amy lowered herself into the one armchair. "That's not quite fair," he said quietly. "If I did word it like that it was because, as soon as he heard my voice, your father said that there was no news of you. That left me with only one other question to ask. Anyway, I was thinking of you and the glider as being a unit – news of one would be news of the other. If the glider was safe, so were you. Of course, if you were safe it didn't necessarily mean that the glider was safe and I don't think you can blame me for wondering if you'd bent it. I'd have deserved it for bashing up your dad's glider anyway."

"Tony, you're babbling."

"Am I? I don't really know what I'm saying." He turned his head away from her. "I thought I'd lost you. But whatever we had together I suppose I've lost it for ever. I seem to have done everything wrong."

She looked at him searchingly. She could only see part of his face, but his body language said it all. He was so obviously woebegone that she knew he was not putting on an act. "Nonsense!" she said briskly. "If anyone got it wrong, I did. I should have read the weather better and have had more sense than to take off with the electronics not working. It wasn't your fault that the battery was flat, was it?"

He faced her again. "In point of fact, no," he said. "That's one thing which, in all honesty, I can put down to somebody else. One of the competitors told me that Julia What's-her-name was seen fiddling about in the cockpit.

I taxed her with it and at first she tried to deny it and then she blew her top. Her fiancé overheard the row. Well, so did everybody else within a mile or more. I suspect that he recognised the tone of voice which she only uses when she's lying her head off. In the end, he made her admit that she'd switched on the variometer. She didn't mean you any real harm," Tony said anxiously. "It was only meant to be a prank – she didn't know enough to realise just how serious it could become. Anyway, Croll read her the riot act and he's going to make her come to Norway with him, towing my trailer, to fetch the glider back. He's a gentleman."

Amy could see that Tony was smarting, perhaps with good cause. "And you fetched my Dad's car and the remains of his glider back to him. That was good of you. What about the Range Rover?"

"I'm flying back to fetch it tomorrow."

"Would you like me to come with you?"

"If you like."

"That's all right, then."

He sighed. "I suppose so."

It seemed to Amy that they had been grumbling at each other for long enough. "I'm sorry if I cost you your chance of a few awards," she said. "Your glider's all right apart from a few slight scuff-marks and some cattle-poo under the starboard wing-tip and you're getting it fetched back for you. So what are you being such a misery about?"

"Nothing."

Having paid Tony back with interest for his patronising and selfish behaviour over the gliding, she had quite forgiven him and her old, slightly maternal, affection

Gerald Hammond

for him was surfacing again. "Come on, Tony," she said. "This is me, remember? I'm the girl who put a fish-hook into your ear and we dumped each other in the pool. We've been friends a long time and we've always been frank with each other. You can tell me. Remember, a trouble shared is a trouble doubled."

Tony refused to laugh. Instead, he sighed again. "Do you mind if I have a drink?" He nodded towards the cupboard holding the mini-bar.

"You're not driving are you?"

"Not until tomorrow night. I came up by train."

"Go ahead, then. I think that the telly people are picking up the bill. I could use something myself after all the excitement."

Tony got up and stooped over the mini-bar. "What would you like?"

"I don't know. Choose me something."

"There's a quarter-bottle of Champagne."

"That'll do. Then you can sit down and unbosom yourself."

Tony poured the Champagne into a beer-glass, helped himself to a miniature of Scotch, added a dash of soda and returned to his seat on the edge of the bed, but instead of drinking he looked down into the glass as if into a bottomless pit.

"Come on," Amy said. "Cough it up and you'll feel better."

Tony forced a small smile. "Can't you let a man be depressed if I want to be?"

"Not if he's an old friend."

"Am I an old friend, Amy?"

"Of course." Amy saw that there were tears in Tony's eyes. She moved to sit beside him on the bed and put an arm round his shoulders. "Come on, what's it about?"

Tony shot the contents of his glass into his mouth and threw the glass across the room. It bounced on the carpet and refused to break. "I've blown it," he said huskily.

"Blown what?"

"Just about everything. Dad's given me an ultimatum. In two weeks, I've got to take over as manager and start commissioning the new unit. I've had my year off and I haven't written a word worth reading. And it's not that I can't write, it's that I can't think of a damn thing worth saying that hasn't been said before."

"There must be lots of plots for a spare-time writer in the world of big business," Amy suggested.

"It's not only that. Also, I thought that I might be impressing you by scoring well at the gliding. Next thing I know you've written a book which has gone straight to the top of the lists and you've shattered some sort of gliding record and you're appearing on television and carrying it off better that I could ever have done – you put that sadistic bugger Davidson firmly in his place, I was watching it in the public bar and they all cheered – and I got carried away and behaved like a stupid bastard and put you off me for all time."

"*No!*" said Amy.

"Yes I have." Tony put his face down on her shoulder. His voice was choked. "You could have told me about the book. You've just said that we've always been frank with each other."

"There was a reason. Someday I'll explain."

209

"You don't have to. Explanations aren't necessary between friends. You're the only person I think of as a real friend. You're a girl and you're younger than I am but – isn't it odd? – I've always looked up to you. And, yes, tried to impress you. And some mess I've made of it!"

Amy felt him sob and at the same moment realised that her shoulder was becoming damp. She turned and put both arms round him, hugging him like a baby. "It's all right," she said.

"But it *isn't* all right. I've made up my mind. I'm not going to take Dad's job. I'm going away."

Amy tightened her grip. "Where to?"

"I don't know. But I don't think I can do the damn job. I'd be tolerated because my father's the boss. I just know that I've got to do something for myself. And when I've found it and done it, I'll come back, I promise."

"Of course you can do the job," Amy said hotly. "You're just suffering from what Dad calls a sag in the self-esteem. The Harvard School of Business is better than anywhere except maybe Zurich, Dad says, and you wouldn't have romped through their MBA Program if you weren't brilliant at money and organising things. And it isn't as if you were joining something that was already up and running. The staff you take on will find you already in the job – so as far as they're concerned you'll be the Big Cheese from Day One." She gave him a little shake. "Just don't let them see you like this."

They sat quietly. He had half-turned and put an arm round her waist.

Amy experienced a rush of emotions but she kept control of herself. Two of them bubbling all over the bedclothes would be too much. His confidence, she could see now, had been reduced to a dangerously low level. From his self-doubts his tendency to put on airs had always sprung. And she had been largely at fault. Her father had tried to warn her.

"Tony," she said gently. "You don't have to go away."

"Yes I *do!*"

"No. You're depressed and you've lost your confidence because of all this, most of which was my fault anyway. A few years' experience bossing around a small unit of three or four accountants plus odds and sods is just what you need to ready you for taking over the whole caboodle."

"You could probably do it better than I could."

Amy nearly lost patience with him but sought for a line of argument which would raise him again in his own estimation. Only one came to her mind. "Now, that's absolute bloody nonsense," she said. "Listen. If I give you a plot which would set you on the road as a writer, will you go along with your father's job?"

"If," he said. "Yes. All right."

"Treat it as a novel or as a piece of investigative journalism or even as what they call faction, I don't mind. Are you ready?"

She felt him nod.

"Listen carefully and take it all in, because I don't think I could bring myself to say it all again. I've been an idiot too. This is what really happened."

Quietly and dispassionately she told the story. She told him of her discussions with Derek Cardinal and his request to let him hide behind her identity. She told him why she had proposed their visit to the Soaring Championships.

And she told him all about her landing on the tanker. As she spoke, she began to see the funny side of the story and she made sure to bring out the Irishness of the tanker crew, the Norse stolidity and kindness of the farmer and the eccentricity of the television team. Only at the end, when she spoke of the writer living out his last hours in Intensive Care did sadness return for a moment.

"All along," she finished, "I've been on the point of owning up to both things, but people, especially Harold Davidson and that horrid man Dunn, kept putting my back up. Why would somebody go out of his way to sabotage a member of the same Association?"

"Money, probably," Tony said.

"If anyone had asked me sympathetically what really happened, I'd probably have told them."

When she stopped speaking, there was silence. At last, Tony got up and walked around the small room. He drew back the curtains and stood looking out of the window. At last he closed the curtains, came back and held her again. They kissed without passion. "You'd be breaking your promise to Derek Cardinal," he said.

"This is more important. And I don't think he's ever going to know."

"And to the tanker crew."

"They're all scattered by now. Anyway, they shouldn't have been messing up the environment."

"You might have to give the money back."

"Cheap at the price."

"You'd be humiliated," Tony said. "People would laugh at you behind your back."

"I can take it."

"I probably couldn't," he said frankly. "But that just goes to show that you have more moral fibre than I have."

"Rubbish!" she said.

"You'd go through all that for me?"

They sat in silence again, holding each other. Amy wondered whether she really could face up to the world if the world knew her for a fraud. She could feel again the upwelling of the deep feelings which she had been slow to recognise until Derek Cardinal had evoked them so movingly in the book. "All that and more," she whispered.

Tony stirred. He detached himself gently and went into the bathroom. She heard water run. He came back and knelt at her feet. She took his cold face in her hands and pulled it against her.

"I couldn't do it to you," he said. His voice was muffled against her breast. "It's enough for me to know that you didn't write the book and didn't fly all the way to Norway. I guess I'll just have to settle for becoming a Captain of Industry and hope that you're right about there being a myriad plots in the world of business."

Amy took a deep breath of relief. She could afford to be generous. "Write under my name if you want to," she said. "After all this hoo-ha it should be a short cut to the bestseller list. Unless you want to be the famous author and be interviewed on television, but I'll tell you for nothing that it isn't all it's cracked up to be. Cheer up, now. You'll be at the Hall and I'll be next door," Amy pointed out. "We'll still be neighbours."

"We could be closer than that," Tony said. "I'm getting

that private flat at the Hall. You could still have a share in your father's business and take over when he wants to retire."

She gave him a little shake. "Tony! You're not making yourself very clear. Are you asking me to move in with you?"

"Yes. More than that, even."

Amy could only imagine one greater step. "You're talking *marriage?*"

Tony pulled her closer. "Yes, of course I am. Why do you think I'm down on my knees? Didn't you know that that was all I ever wanted?"

Amy found a paper handkerchief and blew her nose. "You weren't exactly explicit on the subject," she said through the tissue.

"I'm being explicit now." He looked up and smiled. "Do you remember? Being married and having children was one of the first things you were looking forward to."

"Fancy you remembering that. What were the others?"

"Prime minister. Going into politics, are you?"

"Not in a million years. I'm not politically correct. That's what they'll say when they comment on the Davidson show."

"Politicians are the last people to be politically correct." Tony's voice was still husky but he was recovering his humour. "Listen to them some time. Then you were going to be queen. Let's see. I'm nine million, three hundred and twenty-five thousand, eight hundred and sixty-fourth in line for the throne, so given a nuclear war followed by bubonic plague you might make it yet."

Inwardly, Amy rejoiced to see the old Tony making a comeback. "On the whole," she said, "I think I'd rather be God. Less responsibility. That was my final ambition."

"Is God a meteorologist?"

"Yes, of course he is. Or probably she. The quick and easy way to influence history is through the weather. How have the great events in the world been shaped? By storms – remember the Spanish Armada? By climatic changes—"

"Extinction of the dinosaurs," Tony said. "And drought—"

"Plagues of Egypt. Rain—"

"Noah's flood," Tony said.

"There really was a flood but it was only in the Black Sea and it was more probably due to melting of the polar ice-caps and never mind what it says in the Old Testament. Thunder and lightning."

She waited hopefully, but Tony found himself unable to think of any cataclysmic events triggered by either. He was still on his knees but they had managed to become entwined together. He looked at his watch and pulled apart. "Good God! We've talked half the night away. I'll let you think it over and you can give me your answer in the morning. I'd better go and see if they can let me have a room."

"I'll give you my answer now," Amy said. She took a deep breath. "You don't have to get another room, you can stay here. I said I'd tell you when I was ready and I think I'm ready now. In fact, I know I am."

"Oh, Amy!" Lost for words, Tony clutched her again.

"There's just one thing," Amy said. "Don't be too rough

215

with me. I don't know how it came about, but I'm still a virgin."

Tony backed off a little and looked at her. "As you said, we've always been frank with each other, so I may as well tell you. I'm not."

"I thought you probably weren't. There was a girl in America. I could tell from your letters. Or was there more than one?"

"Just one. It wasn't anything important, to either of us. And – it sounds grisly to say it aloud – I made damn sure I didn't catch anything. We said goodbye as friends and that was it, and she started setting her cap at a department store manager from Ohio. I wouldn't have wanted it to go on any longer. She was a silly sort of a girl, really. Attractive, but silly. A mind full of candy-floss."

"More attractive than me? Even with my hair all over the place?"

"Not by a mile," Tony said fervently. "And not half as bright. Do you mind about her?"

"There wasn't anybody after you came back to Britain?"

He shook his head violently. "Good God no! I had offers, but you were there to compare them with and they didn't stand a chance."

For once he had managed to say the right things for several minutes on end. Perhaps he was learning. Amy pondered the question while rubbing the back of his neck. "No, I don't really mind," she said at last. "Or not a lot. Maybe it was just as well. One of us had better know what he's doing. Just don't let's even mention it again. Let me up. I'll go and undress in the bathroom."

"No." He tightened his hold on her. "You're giving me

an early wedding present. But what's the most fun about presents?"

"Unwrapping them?" Amy said slowly.

"Exactly."

She laughed shakily. "The present itself can be the most awful disappointment."

"Not this time," he said. "Not ever."

"I hope not." She smiled into his eyes, then pushed him gently away and stood, holding up her hands. "All right, Tony."